Seasoned

A Vintage Love Story
with Modern-Day Flavor

Jayme H. Mansfield

LPC Books
Imprint of Iron Stream Media

SEASONED BY JAYME H. MANSFIELD
LpcBooks
a division of Iron Stream Media
100 Missionary Ridge, Birmingham, AL 35242

ISBN: 978-1-64526-275-6
Copyright © 2020 by Jayme H. Mansfield
Cover design by Elaina Lee
Interior design by Karthick Srinivasan

Available in print from your local bookstore, online, or from the publisher at:
ShopLPC.com

For more information on this book and the author, visit: www.jaymehmansfield.com

This is a work of fiction. Names, characters, and incidents are all products of the author's
imagination or are used for fictional purposes. Any mentioned brand names, places, and
trademarks remain the property of their respective owners, bear no association with the
author or the publisher, and are used for fictional purposes only.

All Scripture quotations, unless otherwise indicated, are taken from the Holy Bible,
New International Version®, NIV®. Copyright ©1973, 1978, 1984, 2011 by Biblica, Inc.™.
Used by permission of Zondervan. All rights reserved worldwide. www.zondervan.com.
"NIV" and "New International Version" are trademarks registered in the United States
Patent and Trademark Office by Biblica, Inc.™.

Brought to you by the creative team at LPCBooks:
Yvonne Lehman and Denise Loock

Library of Congress Cataloging-in-Publication Data
Mansfield, Jayme H.
Seasoned / Jayme H. Mansfield 1st ed.

Printed in the United States of America

PRAISE FOR *SEASONED*

Jayme Mansfield does not disappoint. I wondered if she could raise the bar after *Rush* and *Chasing the Butterfly*, and she did not let me down. *Seasoned* is not only timely but also tender and sensitive. She treats the subject of being widowed as sweet as honey on bread. Her story brings hope for new love after devastating loss.

~ **Cindy Sproles**
Best-selling Author of *Mercy's Rain, Liar's Winter,* and
What Momma Left Behind

This masterfully written novel is a heartfelt reminder that it's never too late—and we're never too old—for love. Jayme Mansfield reminds us unexpected love is extra sweet, and, no matter our age, it heals the oldest of wounds and hurts. You'll be touched by this story as you read it, and you'll never forget it.

~ **Henry McLaughlin**
Award-winning Author of *Journey to Riverbend*

Seasoned isn't a love story. It's a human story. Two retirees meet each other through an online dating service. They meet and then cautiously advance into companionship and courtship. It isn't until they are deep into the relationship that they realize their paths aren't disparate, but convergent. Six decades ago, their lives influenced each other in profound, impactful ways, and this is where the story takes on depth.

Jayme Mansfield has the ability to not just tell a tale but to reflect on the human struggle. It's easy to see yourself in the characters of *Seasoned*. In age, I'm several decades removed from the main characters. But in my human condition, I'm right there with them. I wrestle with the failures of the past. And I mourn for relationships that have gone astray. Each character carries a lifetime of separate memories. Each of them carries secret shame and guilt, the sad reminders that tethered them to the past. Unable to move forward, they each find freedom through the power of forgiveness and grace.

The characters reflect our shortcomings as humans—lies, deceit, shame, and guilt. But then bursting onto the pages are the beautiful moments of beauty, forgiveness, and restoration.

To call this a romance is to shortchange the vivid personalities, the playful dialogue, and the moving narrative. This is simply great storytelling.

This work will find appeal across many audiences. Our society is aging, with life expectancy steadily increasing. The truth that many older people face is their partner won't always live the same number of years. The book respectfully deals with the march of time and yet gives deep deference to tender hearts that really never get too old.

It's a sweet story. It's a reminder of grace. It's a tale about second chances to love and to be loved. It's a reminder that it's never too late to start happily ever after. And, more importantly, it's never too late to start living the truth.

~ **David Rupert**
Patheos Featured Writer
Author of *Living a Life of Yes: How One Word Changes Everything*
Founder and Director of Writers on the Rock

Seasoned is a love story for the ages—and for any age. Author Jayme Mansfield is a master storyteller and a true artist when it comes to creating characters who stay with us. This book is destined to become a classic, and I'm already compiling a list of people to whom I'll be sending a copy.

~ **Edie Melson**
Author
Co-director of the Blue Ridge Mountains Christian Writers Conference

A sweet, *Seasoned* romance brimming with love, laughter, and the gift of forgiveness.

~ **DiAnn Mills**
Best-selling Author
Co-director of the Blue Ridge Mountains Christian Writers Conference

Essie is widowed. Because her daughter thinks she might be lonely, Essie is nudged into signing up on a dating site, though she wonders who would want an 80-year-old. Lou, also widowed, is dared by a friend to sign up for the same site, so he does, but under a different name—just in case things don't go well. After all, who would want an 82-year-old? You'd think that this lead-in would end in happily ever after—and it does—but not until several secrets, anxieties, and misunderstandings are resolved. The story of Essie and Lou shows that being brave enough to be truthful can open your heart to love, no matter your age.

~ **Jan Aleksiewicz**
Senior Events Specialist for Adults and Seniors, Arapahoe Libraries

ACKNOWLEDGMENTS

My heartfelt thanks to the following:
Lighthouse Publishing of the Carolinas and Iron Stream Media for believing in me and elevating my writing.

A tremendous thank-you to my general editor and stellar writing mentor, Yvonne Lehman. You recognized the potential in Seasoned with the Golden Leaf Award at the Blue Ridge Autumn in the Mountains Novelist Retreat. You then challenged me to take the story to a higher level, and for that I am grateful.

Copy editor Denise Loock, your expertise at weeding out the unnecessary and adding richness to the prose is extraordinaire. Thanks for the reminder that writing lessons never end.

To my agent, Diana Flegal, your support, wisdom, and friendship are treasured.

Acclaimed artist and friend Kelly Berger, again your talent graces the cover of another of my books—proof that we were sisters separated at birth, reunited, and now melded together through our creative passions.

And, of course, to my husband, James, and my family … you understand that, besides you, my favorite companions are the characters I create and the adventures they take in those dreamy places. Thanks for encouraging me to journey near and far.

For my mother, Janet, who dared to love again.

And for Frank, who brings her flowers and showers her with love.

The two of you are an inspiration ... a reminder that love knows no age.

Chapter One

Essie ~ The Box, 2006

As a prelude to autumn, the Colorado mountain air chilled and the aspens shimmered with gold. I opened the cedar chest to take out my beige sweater to wear for this *meeting* with my daughter, Allie. Over the phone last night, she declared, "Mom, tomorrow is a new day for you."

But my hands betrayed me. I lifted the cardboard box marked ESTHER OWENS WHITE—PERSONAL and set it on the floor. The container weighed more than I remembered. Memories—odd and abstract—fleeting as they slip through my fingers like sand. Others ingrained, deeply cut, scarring. Happy or sad. Light and airy or heavy and dank. Maybe the box seems heavier because it reminds me a broken heart never completely mends.

No, I won't open it. This is a new day. I won't slip on my wedding ring and read through years of anniversary cards. No giggling at family photos, especially the Polaroid of the four of us—my bouffant hairstyle dwarfing our two young kids. No time to flip through the chronology of school photos and … the forty-year-old newspaper clipping of our son's obituary. The yellowed piece of paper isn't needed to remind me of the death of our son, Reece.

I returned the box to the chest and gently covered it with a plaid Pendleton blanket, tucking the past away. Then, ruffling through sweaters, I chose a pretty butter-yellow cashmere and shut the lid. What has my romance-writing daughter, Allie, cooked up? Definitely not food.

Allie said I need to get out more, with a man.

Me … date?

At my age? Ha!

But, if I pretend to go along with this, maybe Allie will use her far-reaching imagination in those fiction stories, not on me.

* * * * *

So, on this Saturday morning, when sensible widows in their eighties would still be in bed, or at least at home in slippers and a robe, I drove the quick fifteen minutes to Allie's to discuss this plan of hers. What do I have to lose? Of course, I have no intention of marrying again after fifty-six years with Ray. Perhaps some friendly socializing wouldn't hurt. After all, my tennis partner, Marge, married and moved to Florida. Phyllis is dating a man she met at the Y, and Carla is in heaven.

I parked in the driveway, stopped to admire the pink sedum overflowing onto the brick walk, and stepped inside. As usual, a soothing concoction misted from the oil diffuser on her writing desk. No-nonsense coffee aroma wafted from the kitchen. For Allie, the perfect atmosphere was as important as hitting the ground running, or writing, that is.

"Hey, Mom." She sipped coffee from the *Happily Ever After* mug I'd given her last Christmas. The moment I looked at her, I knew something wasn't exactly happy for her this morning.

"Give me a sec to finish this sentence." She motioned to the cup and saucer on the corner of her desk. "Here, I have your tea ready. Chamomile. Calm is good, right?"

Before she diverted her gaze back to the computer screen, I spotted her puffy eyelids. Like my own, they were a shared genetic giveaway she'd been crying. And perhaps because my daughter was an author, she was an open book—or at least to me as her mother. But she needed to ease into the initial scene when it involved her personal life. I'd learned to respect that and would wait until she was ready to share.

"There, nailed it." She leaned back in her chair. "This manuscript is a tough one. These characters are making me work for my money."

"Do I get to read it before you send it to your publisher?"

"If you want, but you're an awful editor. You think everything I write is perfect."

"True. That's my mom-job."

"Pretty much the same romance formula. Heroine meets hero, they dig each other but can't show it or don't know it, at least not yet. Then, oh no, a big problem arises and lots of little ones. But they're crazy for each other and things get steamy. More problems, but finally—"

"They make the commitment to spend their lives together, expecting to live happily ever after." Those words always make me smile, and I couldn't help but grin. "As life should be."

Allie gave the universal thumbs-up and changed the subject. "Mom, I'm proud of you for agreeing to this early morning meeting. Shows you still have the get-up-and-go spirit."

"Thanks. I suppose I've never been one to let grass grow around my toes." I fidgeted with my tea bag, lifting, then submerging it again. "So, this plan of yours—"

The topic got a brief reprieve when Snow White, Allie's Westie bounded through the mini-dog door with a stuffed teddy bear in her mouth.

"Whatcha got, Snowy? A new toy?" I patted her head before she gave the bear a vigorous shake and ran from the room. "What's up with her today? She's so spunky."

"Dogs read our emotions. She's as excited as I am about this."

"The plan?"

"Absolutely. The Passion Plan." Allie removed her glasses and nested them atop her head. "Makes it sound more intriguing."

"Hold on a minute. I'm only considering this for companionship. You know, dinner or a movie, maybe catching a museum exhibit or concert."

"Fine. Nix the sex, keep it G-rated."

"Well," I mused, "at least not X-rated."

"Mom!" Allie's eyebrows rose.

"I'm not dead for heaven's sake." I smiled. Giving Allie a bit of her own medicine was fun. *But I could never even kiss another man.*

Allie focused on the computer screen. "It's simple. We should have done this online dating months ago."

"But isn't there an age limit? The market must be tight for eighty-year-olds."

"Maybe slim, but plenty of older people are lonely and know how good it is to be loved—"

"And love." A familiar pang tapped on my heart.

I missed Ray's steady, calming voice when worry crept in. I missed his kiss when he left for work, and again when he returned home at night. I missed his touch. My bed had been so warm when my husband lay by my side as the Colorado snow swirled outside.

Yes, to be loved and to love is bliss—a two-sided coin—each side worthy and necessary. Husband and wife. Mother and child.

Emotions threatened. I should not have touched that box this morning. Sipping the tea, I forced my mind to settle on the husband-and-wife theme.

I swallowed the last drop and set the cup on the desk. "So, how are you and Peter? Is he here?"

Allie gave me a sideways glance. "We're fine. He left early for work." She swiped her hand at the air, dismissing the topic of her personal life. "Anyway, we're focusing on you."

I pressed my lips together in an effort to remain silent, but my instinctual I-know-there-is more-to-the-story slipped out as "Mmm."

"Mom." Allie rolled her eyes. "I wish you wouldn't do that."

"And I wish you wouldn't do this." I rolled my eyes.

"Fair." She grinned.

"Back to the plan." She tapped a series of keys and turned the computer screen toward me. It glowed as if it shared her enthusiasm for whatever she had devised.

"I'm not sure I like what you're up to." I squinted at the words she typed into the Search bar. "And your father would feel the same."

"Dad wouldn't want you to be alone either." She tapped the logo emblazoned on the screen, Liaison. "Besides, we're only looking for a friend … right?"

"Right. No man to pocket my money or have me iron shirts. And if he's my age, there's a good chance he would expect me to push him around in a wheelchair. Let's try to avoid that." I crossed my arms. "Now, if you can find me a handyman to fix everything breaking at my house, that could be an added bonus."

"You're acting a little self-centered, don't you think?"

"Not at all. I'm an octogenarian … but don't you think a man would expect me to cook for him?"

"You like to cook," Allie shot back.

"Not really. I've gotten used to eating light. Something liberating about having a bowl of cereal or popcorn for dinner. I cooked my share of meals over the years, and I don't know if I want to—"

"Mom." Allie pointed at me. "This is only about friendship with a man."

My fingers tapped out a rhythm on my knees. "That's why this idea makes me jittery. Maybe I shouldn't have come." I straightened my back and tried to redirect my attention to the computer. "I know you mean well, but I'm fine. You say you and Peter are fine. Let's agree that everyone's fine and leave well enough alone." I stood. "Do you want more coffee?"

"You're stalling." Allie patted the seat of my chair. "This won't hurt a bit."

Hurt had been part of my subterranean repertoire for so long—coursing through my being like an underwater river and often surfacing where the earth was dry and cracked. However, I'd done a pretty good job taming the water since Ray passed, made respectable progress in healing the wound, especially over the last year. For a long time after he was gone, every day was painful … holidays, birthdays, our anniversary … really any ordinary day.

I'd sat alone at church, received junk mail addressed to Raymond White, and warmed my body with an extra blanket instead of his touch. All acute reminders that he was gone. They still come—like the thieves who unlatched the door to my soul and stole my joy the day my son died.

"I've checked several sites, and this one is the best." Allie clicked on a tab, and a screen full of smiling faces appeared, several cheek-to-cheek and some lip-to-lip.

"Must be the paid testimonials." I leaned closer toward the beaming, white-teethed, pretty people. "I don't see any close to my age. Must be an age cap."

"Sorry. No such thing. You could be over a hundred and join." Allie clicked another icon, and a form with numerous blank spaces appeared. "This is where we start. A new chapter for a wonderful woman, looking for fun and companionship with a man who wants the same."

"But look at this." I pointed to a row of boxes. "They want to know my age, where I live, my hobbies. They're awfully nosy, don't you think?"

"Unless you'd like to meet a man half your age, living in Hawaii, who likes to surf naked, then I'd say this is all pretty reasonable to find a good match." Allie began to fill in the blanks.

"Hmm. Naked surfing. Sounds dangerous."

"Could be worse … naked skydiving … sword fighting." She continued typing. "This is the basic profile information. The probing goes much deeper."

"Honey." I paused, allowing my words to catch up with my heart.

"Do I deserve another special person in my life? I had your father, a wonderful son, and I'm blessed to have you. I'm not sure that I'm worthy of more."

There, I'd said it. My response surprised me. *Gratitude.* Self-help proponents shout it from the mountaintops—staying focused on what was and is good in life is the answer to all the world's problems. Perhaps my gratitude cup overflowed long ago. And yet, I thought as I glanced at the empty teacup, maybe there is such a thing as a second serving.

Allie closed her eyes and took a deep breath before she spoke. "Not having Dad the last two years has been tough. I miss him too. But life was never meant to be—"

"Lived in a box?"

Allie's shoulder's slumped. "Right. Not lived in a box."

I nodded. Surprisingly, agreeing felt good.

"You're an amazing woman, ready for a positive change. Mom, maybe someone out there would make you happy. Maybe someone needs you."

Such a complex concept ... to be needed. I'd been needed for so long. First, a young nurse out of college, then a wife, soon after a mother, later on a caregiver when Ray's heart was failing. Like a chocolate cream cake, multiple layers, all necessary to complete the richness of my life. But an essential part of the cake crumbled when Reece died, and more fell away after Ray passed.

Wasn't that how every love story eventually ended? Widow? Widower?

But ... could there be a man out there, wherever out there is, who might need me? Someone who enjoys good, intelligent conversation that's different than girl-to-girl or guy-to-guy talk? Another person who wants to feel special again without having to get married? Someone who gets the "been there, done that" thing?

After a deep breath, I said, "I'll agree to try this only if I can back out when I want. Stop any time, pretend the whole thing didn't—"

"Mother, must I remind you that I'm a romance writer?" A sly smile crept across her face. "You are in good hands. Allie LaFleur is your official online dating ghostwriter."

"And I'm supposed to feel so much better?" I grinned. It was time for me to have a little fun as well, and weaving relationships, albeit fictional, was right up Allie's alley.

"This will be a blast! After we input your basic information and the matches start to come in, I'll log in as you and do all the writing."

"And what do you plan to say to these gentlemen, if any respond?"

"I'll tell them how fascinating and full of life I—I mean *you* are. That you're now a widow, after being happily married for many years, and simply looking for another man to spend quality time with."

"And fix the screen door that won't shut." I pointed to the keyboard. "Don't forget the handyman part."

"Mom, this isn't a classified ad for home repair."

"Well, that's a good reason for having a man at my house."

Her eyes softened. "You are lonely … and no one should be lonely."

I stared into my daughter's hazel eyes, reminiscent of her father's. She was right. Could the truth overrule my pride, and more accurately, my fear? The fear that, like the sands of time, my opportunity to love and be loved had disappeared?

No, I still have time on my side. I hovered my fingers and air-typed. "Then, my dear, make me fascinating."

"You *are* fascinating. And remember, I'm a writer. I can handle this." Allie set her fingers on the keyboard and typed, Esther White.

"My formal name instead of Essie? Sounds a bit mysterious. I like that. Haven't used it in years."

"Good. Next, what should your password be?"

"I need a password to meet a man?" I scoffed. "That sounds complicated."

"How about the movie *Sleepless in Seattle*, and we can make the *s*'s dollar signs? I love when Tom Hanks meets Meg Ryan on top of the Empire State Building." Allie patted her heart.

"I thought our goal was companionship."

"It is." She sighed. "But that scene is hard to beat."

"Agreed."

Allie logged in and entered her credit card information. "Since it was my idea and I'm dragging you into this, I'll pay." She eyed me. "If you get hooked and men are waiting in droves to wine and dine you for months, then you're picking up the ongoing fee."

"Don't hold your breath. I hardly think my demographics will result in a flood of suitors." I offered my hand. "For this arrangement to be fair, I have a bet to make with you."

"And what would that be?"

"I agree to give online dating a whirl if you tell me what's going on with you and Peter." A loose strand of hair had slipped from her ponytail, and I tucked it behind her ear as I had done hundreds of times when she was a child. "Even if you say everything is fine, I still have a suspicion, call it mother's intuition, that things aren't going according to your desired storyline … plus, your eyelids are puffy."

Allie lowered her head. "Where do I begin?"

"Where most authors begin … with chapter one."

Chapter Two

Lou ~ A Dare

Like clockwork, my phone rang at eleven a.m. on Sunday morning. "Hey, doll," I said, as I silenced my CD player and cut Pavarotti in mid crescendo. I never tire of hearing my daughter's voice.

"Hi, Daddy. How you feeling today?" She tried, but Jennifer couldn't mask the perpetual concern in her voice.

"Like a spring chicken." My autopilot response never derailed her weekly interrogation. It doesn't help that I'm eighty-two-years-old and live on my own outside of Denver, far from her Manhattan apartment. When her mom died and I lost my wife of fifty-eight years, I earned one of the top slots on Jennifer's concern list. I'm thankful she cares, but I've never been one that likes to be fussed over.

"Seriously. Have you taken your blood pressure medicine and done your stretches this morning?"

"Of course. How could I miss the giant day-of-the-week pillbox you ordered online? I considered a part-time job at the VA hospital to help distribute meds to the entire psych wing with it."

An audible sigh followed on the other end of the line.

"Just kidding, hon. I feel great."

Lately, my memory isn't as sharp … but I remember the good stuff, like when Betty and I finally had our two kids out of the nest and we holed up in the house and didn't come out for a week. We even made love in the living room, bumping into the card table and knocking the nearly completed, one-thousand-piece puzzle of Mount Rushmore on to the shag carpet. We laughed until we cried.

"And I'm about to stretch. Just ran sprints around the block."

Her quick intake of breath indicated I'd pushed her too far. "You did not. Tell me you're kidding."

"Jennifer, I'm fine, and no, I didn't run around the neighborhood … although it'd be fun to see if I can still do it. Your mom and I loved our evening jaunts—I tell you, that little lady had a clip to her step. But I did take my morning spin on the stationary bike and clocked in just over an hour. Impressive, don't you think? The Tour de France may be in my future." I chuckled.

What I didn't share was that by seven a.m., I'd already been out of bed three times, twice to pee and once to double-check the back door was locked. Twenty-nine years in the active Army taught me to never leave my backside vulnerable. What it hadn't covered was how to age gracefully.

Jennifer sighed. She and my son-in-law, even though they're empty nesters, don't seem to laugh as much as they once did. Carl's multiple sclerosis is becoming more obvious, and Jennifer is scared, not only for her husband but also for her future as well. Maybe she's scared of losing me too, and that's why she fusses over me.

"Well, I have good news," Jennifer spoke loudly into the phone.

Probably thinks my hearing is failing.

"We're coming to Colorado for Christmas. Carl wants to take Matt and Kristi skiing in Vail while they're on semester break. Since they're at separate colleges, it's even harder for our family to be together."

"But I bet you and Carl are enjoying the freedom with no kids in the house." I smiled to myself. "Sorry to break the news, but your mom and I loved that time we had together after you left for college."

"That was you and Mom. Carl and I have such full schedules. It's not like all of a sudden he and I intersect in some amazing way."

"Well, you're married for Pete's sake. The two of you should—"

"Dad, we're talking about the vacation. Not my marriage."

I know Jennifer well, and when she shortens the endearing Daddy to Dad, she's not messing around. My usual fatherly advice wasn't welcome, at least on this subject. "Carl's up for skiing?"

"Not full days, especially with the high elevation." Jennifer sighed. "But he misses the whole scene, and even if he isn't able to ski like he used to, we'll enjoy the après ski drinks in town. A vacation will be good for the family, and we can spend part of the holiday with you."

"I'd like that, hon." I thought of my good buddy, Hank Lambert. He mentioned he might be spending Christmas somewhere new this year … I'll have to ask him about that. Anyway, if he isn't around, I'd most likely be alone, and it'd be nice to have company and see the grandkids—no longer kids. "Jen, we can talk more next week as your plans come together."

"Daddy, you know we can talk any time. Doesn't have to be only Sunday at eleven."

"I know, but you have your life, and I'm living mine." I paused, wondering if what I said was a half-truth. I took care of the essentials, plus more … eating, sleeping, exercising, challenging my mind on the computer with the stock market, world news, researching genealogy. Always into a good history book too. Even though Betty and I talked a time or two about simplifying and downsizing, even trying a retirement community, I like the familiar space around me. The house suits me fine. I have my daughter on the phone every Sunday morning. And I have my friend, Hank.

But some days I wonder. Am I really living?

* * * * *

Hank comes by every Friday night, and we walk over to Viva Dolce. He gets spaghetti, and I order the lasagna. For years, we went as a foursome with our wives. His Shelly passed away shortly after my Betty. After that, we tried the Chinese restaurant in the same shopping center—thought it might do us good to switch it up, try something new. But after one meal, we stared at each other across a mound of rice and sweet-and-sour pork like two lost kids. We're back to our Italian restaurant with its red and white tablecloths, green Pellegrino bottle in the center holding a red carnation, paper menus stained with wine and food, and two empty chairs.

Before I had a chance to ask about his Christmas plans, Hank told me maybe we should switch to eating lunches on a weekday.

"The lady friend I'm seeing—" He slurped a stray noodle that dangled beneath his mustache.

"Libby."

"Yes." Hank cleared his throat. "We're having lots of fun together." He poked at a meatball. "She likes to go square dancing on Friday nights and needs a partner."

"So do I," I blurted.

"Then come to church with me and meet the ladies. All sorts of widows, and some are lonely. Libby's told them about—"

"You're my partner."

Hank's eyes widened.

"You know what I mean." My fork clanged on the plate. "I haven't gone to Mass since Betty felt well enough to be out of the house. And you know I went only to make her happy. If she hadn't volunteered me for parking lot duty, maybe I would have gotten something out of it."

"Why didn't you catch the later service?"

"We were half frozen by the time all the late-comers arrived, but I was no dummy. Went inside for my free coffee and Danish, and then it was time to help the crowds rush out of the lot."

"Never too late to try again."

"Church?" I smirked. "You make it sound like a dating service."

"I don't know about that." Hank wiped his lips with a sauce-stained napkin. "Never saw much good in church until now, but maybe it's because my own end is in sight." He leaned into the table. "Who are we fooling, Lou? Both of us are ancient by today's standards."

"I'd debate that."

"Okay, ditto." Hank lowered his voice and stared me down. "Regardless, our lives have been blessed. Came home from the wars to good paying jobs and wives who loved us despite ourselves. Call me selfish, but I want to keep living a good life … when this body is dead and gone, I'm holding out there's room for me in heaven."

A long sip of wine gave me time to think. "Hank, you mean well, and I respect you for it. I just don't think it's right for me to waltz into church after all these years and act like I have any business being there."

"We've all made mistakes, hurt people along the way." He cocked his head to fourteen hundred hours and eyed me the way he did when he knew there was more on my mind.

I raised my hand in an attempt to flag down the server, but she sped by in a blur. "Agreed."

"Agreed? That's all you want to say?"

"Yep." I waved my hand again only to receive the customary be-back-in-a-minute nod.

"Well then, I'm happy you agree to accept a dare." He grinned, accentuating the wrinkles framing his blue eyes.

"I have? What have I agreed to?" I slipped a twenty-dollar bill from my wallet. "Maybe the waitress will bring the check when she sees real money. Does anyone carry cash any more except us old guys?"

"Online dating. Liaison. One month." Hank crossed his arms and settled back in his chair as if perched at a high-stakes poker table. "I dare you. I'll even bet you twenty bucks to make it more enticing. The money is yours if you give it a shot, go on some dates, and find someone who is interesting."

"Interesting?" I raised my brow. "Why not someone who wants to keep me warm at night?"

"That would be a bonus. At our age, best to start with interesting."

"Hank Lambert. Even for a good-looking Italian such as myself, your idea to hook me up with a woman is about as silly as that ponytail you're sporting."

"Hey, hey. Go easy on your best friend. The military took my hair for most of my life, and I intend to enjoy the little I have left. Besides, Libby says I remind her of Willie Nelson."

As Hank continued to talk, I couldn't help but acknowledge the resemblance with a quick nod.

"All I know is you're lonely and still have some gas left in you. Libby's brought life back into me, and the right woman might do the same for you."

"I had the right woman." A lump in my throat ambushed me, and I swallowed hard. Hank pushed the noodles around his plate and gave me a moment to regroup.

Finally, I leaned forward and crossed my arms on the table. "Possibly." Now it was my turn to assume the negotiation pose. "What age are we talking here? Forty? Thirty? Younger?"

"That might be a little ambitious, and we need to keep this legal. But I like your spirit. You have plenty of money …"

"A nice house on just shy of an acre, luxury sedan, good pension." I ran my hand through my thick silver hair. "And my good looks caught the girls' attention at the USO shows back in the day."

Hank smirked, and I took that as his acknowledgment that I had turned a head or two.

If Hank could get a woman at his age, why can't I? But for what? Intelligent conversation? Light-hearted laughter? Some handholding and more if the spark is right?

Hesitantly, I extended my hand across the table. "Okay, but make it double … make it forty bucks." As the waitress sped by, she handed off the black vinyl case like a baton in a relay race.

Hank clamped his hand on mine and shook. "Deal. It'll be worth your effort. All you have to do is sign up for a month's subscription. One of Libby's church friends can help you if you want."

"I thought all those ladies found love at church."

"Just like fishing, you do the email correspondence and get as many bites as you can, reel one or two in, and go on some dates. The forty bucks will pay for your first date." Hank spread his arms as if preparing for a gigantic bear hug. "Maybe you'll get lucky and hook the catch of a lifetime."

I gathered my jacket and WWII veteran ball cap from the extra chair. "My friend, I already did and lost her."

I exited the restaurant a bit differently—not with only my usual full belly and empty heart. Instead, my pace felt lighter, a pep in my step that had been absent awhile. Maybe Hank was right. This could be … interesting.

Chapter Three

Essie ~ Dark and Light

I hoped Allie was gathering her thoughts, for at least a prologue, as to what was bothering her when Peter lumbered through the door with his hand clamped over his forehead and face grimacing. Another whopper migraine waylaid him at work—our cue to give him solitude and, instead, talk at my home.

"Do you think we should have left him like that? What if he needed lunch?" A familiar *tsk-tsk* escaped my mouth, and I had to believe the sound originated from a primordial, mothering gene.

"Trust me, he doesn't have an appetite when he feels this way, and the best remedy is to leave him alone and let him sleep." She sighed. "The stress of his new position as department manager must be bringing these on."

"And the bright lighting in the store can't help. Or all those beautiful, flashy shoes."

"I won't stay long." Allie pulsed the blender a final time before pouring a green mixture into our glasses.

I held my glass to the light streaming in my kitchen window and eyed the contents. "What exactly are we drinking?"

"Yogurt, carrots, bananas, and blueberries."

"Then why's it the same color as the kitchen countertops I had in the seventies?"

"That's the spinach." She sipped her drink. "You had a bag in the refrigerator."

"That was for a salad I have to take to the church potluck, not a smoothie."

"Oh well. It's good for you. Makes your heart healthy, your skin glow, and your eyesight better ... or something like that." I followed her through the sliding door leading to my back deck. A fresh blast of early autumn air greeted us.

Breathing deeply, I walked across the wooden platform, overlooking the clusters of brilliant yellow aspen trees tucked between the deep hues of pines. "I love the changing seasons, don't you?"

"Nothing better than watching the landscape change, season after season." Allie rested her elbows alongside mine on the railing. "Time for a beautiful new season for you as well, Mom. I'm proud that you've agreed to try dating."

I patted my daughter's hand. "Allie, your concern is appreciated. But you need to accept I'm getting old." I chuckled. "Not *getting* old. I *am* old."

"You're still breathing, and last time I checked, that means you're alive."

"I didn't say dead—just old. As old as that bent-over pine on the ridge, to the right of that big slab of rock." I pointed to the west where the brilliant blue sky met the wash of yellow leaves. "Stunning, isn't it? Cerulean blue meets cadmium yellow—perfect complements. Dab in hookers and sap green, a little yellow ochre and cad orange, and you have a masterpiece."

"How do you do that?" Allie aligned her left and right forefingers and thumbs to make a tiny frame and peered through her self-made viewfinder. "I can't see any of that. Sure, there are different colors and kinds of trees, the blue sky above"—she lowered her head and slid her hands into her pockets—"but I can't bring it to life like you do."

"Of course you can. Take a look again." I raised my hand above my eyes to shade the sun. "What colors do you see?"

"Yellow and green."

"What else?"

"Blue."

"Where?"

"Up in the sky, of course."

"Only there?" I pointed again.

"Yes."

"Look again. And squint this time."

I studied my daughter as she stared at the hillside of Mount Talon. Despite professionally highlighting her hair with soft shades of blonde and warm tan hues, the hair alongside her temples had grayed when she stepped into her early forties, defying her best attempts to remain forever young.

I understood. For years, my hairdresser dyed my graying hair with an apricot-colored 'do reminiscent of Lucille Ball's. Besides, everyone loved Lucy. But after several years—and the realization that my hairdresser's frosting procedure was making my style look more like the month-old display of cupcakes in the bakery window—I was better off giving my natural silver hair its debut.

"What do you see now?" My arm slipped around Allie's waist.

"Brown."

"What kind of brown?"

"Mom, brown is brown."

"Oh really? How about deep umber and burnt sienna—like chocolate brown and rust? And look at the pine trees. They're not simply green."

"They look green to me. Maybe some brown." She leaned forward. "There's black too … and I know what you're going to say. Black isn't a color."

"Technically correct, but extremely important. Take white or the light areas." I rested on the railing again, and let my eyes wander across the landscape in front of me. "Just like our lives, A forest wouldn't be so amazing without all its darks and lights. It wouldn't have depth and perspective. It wouldn't look … or rather it wouldn't be … alive."

Allie sniffed.

"Are you crying?"

She shook her head at first but then nodded.

"Dear, what's wrong?"

She tried to smile, but her lower lip quivered. "Do you really believe that, Mom?"

"Believe what? The principles of art?"

"No. What you said. That to be alive, we have to have dark and light in our lives." She blinked, her eyes opening wide as they did when she was frightened as a child. "Everyone has difficulties … even really awful times to realize the good in life?"

"Did I say all that?" I raised one brow, wondering why our Bob Ross moment changed so quickly.

"I'm being serious. Answer me, Mom. Why have you always been able to see possibilities, and I only see black and white?"

I made my way to the wrought-iron glider and sat, leaving space next to me. "Sit and talk."

Allie plopped herself on the sun-faded, floral cushion and sighed. "Can we glide first?"

We pushed our bare feet against the wooden planks and moved back and forth in tandem, as if aligning our hearts and minds like mothers and daughters do.

After listening to the chorus of gently rustling leaves and the melodic twang of the rusty glider springs, I spoke. "Yes. Hills and valleys. Dark and light. The necessity of both is the hard truth of life. No fun to talk about, and we surely don't want to live it." We continued in motion. "I do know one thing … without sadness, there's no way to measure joy."

I closed my eyes and let the truth wash over me. I'd known loss and its bedfellows—sadness and depression. During those dark times, I learned a heart could break—a break so painful that the only remedy would be death. But the timing of that final occurrence—my homegoing to the place where those I loved and lost waited for me—would be left to God. And over the years, my passion for art had taught me that a painting is made more rich, interesting, and meaningful with the combinations of light and darks, and so is life. Without the dark, the light is lost.

"If you want to talk about what's bothering you, I'm here to listen." I leaned my head onto my daughter's shoulder. "And if not, we'll just glide."

Allie was quiet for several moments. She twisted her wedding band around her finger until she finally spoke. "It's Peter … and something he told me. This time my story may not end happily ever after."

I was all set to give advice. I've known about those wandering, unfaithful men, and my response could take her into the direction of divorce or forgiveness.

She added, "He's threatening to leave me."

Yes, I'm right. He's having an affair.

But never in my life did I expect what she said next that left me speechless.

"Mom. He says it's because of my"—she huffed out a quick breath, and her eyes flashed—"my unfaithfulness."

Chapter Four

Lou ~ Caught

Go Army, beat Navy! I can chant the words in my sleep, but admittedly, I run a tight ship. Shortly after Betty died, my daughter insisted I hire a cleaning lady, if for no other reason than to water the plants my wife had acquired as if our home was a safe house for abandoned and fledgling botanicals. Regardless, dust and tile mold don't stand a chance in my home on my watch. My housekeeper, Arlene, begs to differ. She's a tough one, and I've wondered if I've met my match.

At first, the idea of a stranger snooping around my mail and rearranging things bothered me. But Arlene and I have found a rhythm. Each Tuesday morning, when she moves to the left, I shift to the right. If she complains about too many picture frames and war medals to dust, I pour her another cup of coffee. When she nags about the closed blinds and the plants' need for natural light, I start into one of my old war stories. On cue, she revs the vacuum and peace is restored.

This morning, she caught me red-handed with Liaison open on my computer screen.

"You've got to be kidding." She tapped the glass with a bright-red fake fingernail. "Are you dating?"

My face must have deepened a shade or two, but I wasn't going to be questioned by a woman half my age, single, and a regular attendee at the Denver's Roundup western dance club.

"Of course not." Before I could maneuver the mouse to blacken the screen, her hand pounced on mine like a cat.

"Not so fast, you sly dog. Looks like you were putting in personal information."

"It's research … for a friend." I scooted my chair closer to the desk, trying to regain my composure. "Helping him out."

"Joseph Marino?" Arlene leaned over my shoulder, her flowery perfume wafting like a giant bouquet. "Who's that?"

"A buddy from the Y." It was against my nature to lie, even a small fib like this one.

"You haven't been to the gym in months."

"And how would you know that?" I followed her eyes to my protruding belly. "It's my love handle." As much as I tried to outsmart Arlene, her puckered lips confirmed she was on to me.

"I see Joseph lives at the same address as you. Hmm? Shares the same email." As she tapped her lips with her forefinger, a vague memory surfaced of being caught by my mother while sneaking into the house late one night.

"Okay, I give." I threw my arms into the air. "But this is all because of Hank."

She stood her ground—a sure sign she demanded more information.

"You would have made a good war interrogator, just like my daughter," I said, trying to lighten the mood.

"Thank you." She smiled, reminding me that as often as I grumbled and accused her of misplacing my car keys or favorite sweater, she'd been one of the few consistent people in my widowed life except for the mailman, my doctor at the VA, and Hank.

Arlene pulled a chair from the kitchen table and settled next to me. "At least you didn't lie about your age. You and Joseph even have the same birthdate."

"All right. I'll come clean. Hank dared me into a one-month subscription for online dating. He knows I'd never turn down a challenge. He has a lady friend from his church, and he's feeling guilty about abandoning his old buddy. Now he's hoping I find a companion, or at least a distraction."

"A distraction from what?" Arlene's eyes sagged too much for one so young, and I realized I'd never asked much about her life. Now her question hung in the air, and I feared the answer.

"Did you hear me, Lou?"

Looking across the room, I locked eyes with Betty, her beautiful face and soft gray curls captive behind the photo frame's glass.

Arlene glanced over her shoulder at the photo propped on the bookshelf, joining my brief reunion with my wife of fifty-eight years.

"You miss her."

"Terribly," I whispered.

Arlene turned toward me, her brow creased with lines of wisdom. "I understand. I really do."

"Do you miss being married?" After knowing her over a year, I felt foolish for not asking sooner.

"In a way, I suppose." She hunched her shoulders and then let them slump as if air had been released from her like a Christmas blow-up decoration soon to be stowed away until the next season.

Odd how memories of Betty ambushed my heart. Christmases with Betty—she loved to decorate for the holiday. Although it cost me a small fortune each year, every added bough, ribbon, and carved angel joining the ever-growing collection made me smile.

Arlene's raspy, cigarette-smoking voice bounced me to the present. "I never talk about it, but he left me for another woman the day after our tenth anniversary. We'd just returned from a beach vacation in Puerta Vallarta. I was tan and feeling beautiful when he said he never really loved me after all."

"Idiot." Something more sensitive would have been nice. *You are beautiful. Or, he made the biggest mistake of his life … or something like that. But that might sound creepy coming from an octogenarian to a woman half my age.*

Arlene must have read my mind. She smirked. "I've called him much worse." She folded the dusting cloth several times, reducing it to a neat square before running it over the computer screen. "That's when I began cleaning houses for a living. My way of keeping order in life."

I chuckled, understanding the need to keep my socks aligned in the drawer by color, toothbrush upright in a clean glass to the right of the bathroom sink, shoes polished, and car washed, even though I had no one to impress.

She stopped mid-swipe and stared at me. "Crazy thing is, I swore I'd never want to love again, but I miss what it's like to love and be loved."

My next words came easily, as if escaping from a deep and raw wound. "I do too."

We nodded in unison—two people from different generations, with different interests and backgrounds, but human beings created to love.

Then, as if there were another sink to clean or load of laundry to run, Arlene thumped me on the shoulder and motioned for me to relinquish my seat.

"Let me get behind the wheel." She slid into the chair, straightened the keyboard, and grabbed hold of the mouse. "Okay, I'm not a big fan of online dating, but let's get this application as juicy and intriguing as possible." She rubbed her palms together and poised her fingers on the keyboard. "Ready, Joe?"

Chapter Five

Allie ~ Gray

I paced the deck, glancing at Mom each time I made an about-face. No doubt, my words shocked her. They even surprised myself—like a defendant confessing to something she didn't do, crumbling under pressure. But for what? Admitting the *possibility* of committing the crime?

Mom sat motionless on the glider, hands folded in her lap, head bowed, most likely praying for my salvation. Maybe I needed it, but then again, what did I believe any more? Fact? Fiction? The line between those worlds was as twisted as a tangled ball of string.

I stopped with my back to her. Perhaps confession would be easier if her eyes couldn't meet mine. "It's not what you're thinking."

No response. I was about to spin around and make sure she was okay when she spoke.

"That's good … I think." She cleared her throat. "I'm listening."

Unfaithfulness. Does it count when another person isn't involved—at least not a *real* person? Peter was right. For the last year, I have spent more time dialoguing with my book characters than talking with him. Their hopes and passions are my bedfellows, as I lie awake devising their next move. I wrestle along with them as anger, sadness, and fear permeate relationships and shatter dreams. Layered within pages of my books are love relationships that are more exciting than mine with my husband. *You're pathetic, Allie. Those people exist only in black and white letters, corralled into words and sentences that communicate action, thought, and deed. None of it is real.*

"Peter thinks I'm having an affair … or more accurately, affairs."

"Is he right?"

"No." I shifted my weight and continued to stare beyond the railing. "Not exactly."

The glider springs twanged, and Mom was at my side. "What's that supposed to mean? Last time I checked, being unfaithful is black or white … not much in the middle."

"How about gray?"

As I faced her, I couldn't ignore the lines of worry and concern crisscrossed on her forehead. They were deeper now, even more defined than when I first noticed them at Reece's funeral … sitting between my mom and dad and watching tears roll down her cheeks.

As the pastor droned on about a loving and comforting God, Daddy held my hand and squeezed it so hard my fingers went numb. But I didn't pull my hand away or say anything—I knew he needed me and I needed him.

Mom had held a crumbled embroidered handkerchief, clutched between her hands and buried in her lap. I wanted her to clasp my other hand and hold as tightly as my dad did. Instead, when her tears wouldn't stop, I wrapped my arm around her neck and held her tight. I vowed never to hurt my mom like Reece did when he went off and died.

"Everything's so confusing." My temples throbbed, and I paused, thinking of my poor husband holed up in the bedroom with his migraine and most likely worrying about work. *I hope he's asleep or at least turned off his cell phone.*

I expected Mom to jump in with an array of questions, but she was silent and nodded as if inviting me to share more.

I continued, "All we do is work. It's been forever since we took a vacation or did something fun together. He says I won't peel myself away from the computer, and I say he's never home anyway. He even used the word *neglected*. Can you believe that?"

When her right eyebrow rose, an unspoken guilt washed over me.

"I promise, I am not, nor would I become, involved with another man … or men for that matter." I propped my hands on my hips in a last-ditch effort to redeem myself. "But am I such an awful and selfish person that my husband is—"

"Lonely?" Her eyes narrowed as if looking into my soul as mothers do. "And maybe you are too?"

I fixed my eyes on hers and summoned the question that had been chasing me in recent nightmares. "Should I give up my writing?"

I didn't expect Mom's quick intake of breath. I especially didn't expect her to pace the deck as I had a few moments ago.

After a few laps, she stopped. "Only if you want to be unfaithful to your calling … to your God-given talent."

I gazed toward the mountain—the blue sky fit like a perfect puzzle piece above the ridge, zigzagged with the silhouette of pointy treetops— and all different shades of light and dark that didn't seem to be there before. "I suppose I've never thought of my writing that way."

I turned and looked at my mother—an older version now of the woman I had journeyed with my entire life—yet just as spectacular and beautiful as the landscape playing out behind me.

"Mom, how do you feel now that you don't paint anymore?"

She was silent, but her face turned ashen gray.

Chapter Six

Essie ~ Strike Three, 2006

Nearly a month into my online dating agreement, Allie called another meeting at her home. This time I wore a bright pink sweater—figured it was about time to step it up a notch despite not having gone on a single date.

Dear Jonathan, I too am fond of birds, particularly the red-breasted robin and …

"Mom, what other kinds of birds do you like?" Allie called as I came out of her kitchen balancing a tray with our turkey sandwiches and diet sodas.

"Why?" I set the tray on the desk and glanced at the screen. "Who is this poor, lonely soul?"

"Jonathan from Parker. He's a bird-watcher."

"As his profession?"

"He's seventy-eight. It's his hobby." Allie handed me the initial correspondence she had printed from a potential match. "He made the cut, so he's in the respond-to file folder."

I scanned the letter and handed it to my daughter. "I'd say it's more like an obsession. These bird names aren't pronounceable. He probably made up half of them to impress someone."

"Give the guy a break. If you read to the end, he says he was a scientist." Allie pointed to the last paragraph. "Ornithologist, see?"

"Bird scientist. No wonder he listed every possible bird in the Northern Hemisphere." My faux tortoise-shell readers hovered on the end of my nose as I leaned toward the screen. "Oh my, you can't say red-breasted robins."

"And why not? They're birds, aren't they?"

"Allie." I tapped a single word on the screen.

"Breasted?"

"He'll get the wrong idea."

Allie snickered. "You've got to be kidding. He's about your age and clearly more interested in birds than anything else."

"Well, I'm not taking any chances." I rubbed my finger across the word on the screen as if it would magically disappear. "Remember, you are only the ghostwriter. The final say is mine." I nodded in agreement with myself. "Plus, we should use an *exotic* bird. Sounds more intriguing, you know, keep him guessing."

"I like your spirit, Mom."

"By the way, you said the bird-watcher made the cut. Are there others?"

Allie opened the manila folder. "Two."

"That's not many." I eyed the thin layer of paper. "Anyone of interest?"

"One is the deaf musician we already talked about. Probably a nice person and a romantic if he plays the violin."

"Isn't he the one who prefers younger women?"

"That's right." Allie crumpled his paper and tossed it in the wastebasket.

"How many didn't make the cut?"

Allie took a long gulp from her soda before replacing it on the tray. "If I recall, one other."

"This isn't hard math." Now it was my turn to take a long drink. "We've only had four matches in nearly a month? What was wrong with the one who got cut?"

"He lives somewhere in Texas, and he's interested in a woman who can drive a tractor."

"I suppose I could do that." I sat back in the chair mentally tallying my poor results. "So much for requesting matches within one hundred miles or less. Thought I was being generous."

"It's not you, Mom." Allie pulled the bottom sheet from the pile. "Your odds go down as your age goes up."

"And up and up and up." Pushing myself from the chair, I gathered my purse from the sofa. "Sweetie, I appreciate what you're trying to do, but I'll be glad when the introductory month is up in a few days and we can forget about all of this."

"You never know what can happen"—Allie squeezed her eyes

shut—"in less than a week."

"What's happened since our talk?" I tossed my purse onto the sofa. "You promised me there wasn't another man and this whole thing between you and Peter was a big misunderstanding … that both of you needed to work less and spend more time together."

Allie walked to the front window and leaned her head against the glass. Usually full of words and wit, she was quiet, contemplative. I waited for her to speak, lingering in a unique place of both mother and friend. Whether your child is five or almost fifty, your hearts are attached. Emotions pulse back and forth, sharing the same pain and intensity as if connected by a live wire.

"That is true. But this week, now that I met my deadline, I've had more time to think." Her face contorted as though the thought cut. "I write about love all day … being in love, falling in love … but I'm not sure what real love is. I'm not even sure if I love Peter."

Her words were faint, and I wondered if I'd heard her correctly. But I knew I did. And although silence is often the best response when someone needs a listening ear, this time my loss for words seemed hollow and fruitless.

Peter was difficult to read early in their relationship. In all fairness to him, his first language was French. My best attempt at the romance language was limited to two years in high school. I learned how to ask about the weather and where to find the nearest bathroom. Hardly romantic. Our talks were shallow at best. But as the years passed and Peter's English developed, with the benefit of an intriguing accent, he was quite charming. In fact, we'd spent many evenings chatting at the kitchen table, well past the cleared dishes and into his second or third cup of coffee—a magical feat on his part.

He talked about realizing his American dream to study in the States and pursue a career in the fashion industry. I wondered if leaving Paris—the fashion capital of the world—and coming to Colorado to study, work various retail jobs, and eventually manage the shoe department at Nordstrom's was what he had in mind.

At family gatherings, he reminded us Allie was his most prized reward for leaving his home on La Rive Gauche near the Sorbonne University. In his heavy accent and with his arm tucked tightly around Allie's waist, he declared, as though for the first time, "I *left* the Left Bank in Paris in search of the *right* girl."

How could she not love him any longer? They were crazy about each other when they got engaged and adventured into the blissful first years of marriage. Even after the miscarriages and the future attempts at getting pregnant. Did something change way back then?

"Mom, did you hear me?" Allie stood in front of me, a hand on each of my shoulders.

"I'm sorry, dear." My incessant blinking must have scared her because she gave me a slight jerk.

"Mom?"

As if shaking away thoughts of the past to make room for the present, I shook my head. "Just surprised … and saddened. But why are you questioning if you love him?"

"It's different now."

"Are you sure?"

Allie resumed her position by the window, slumping her shoulders like a moody teenager. "Pretty close."

"Allie, *pretty close* only counts in horseshoes and hand grenades, not saying you don't love your husband."

"Why are you siding with him?" She shot me a stern glance.

"If he's guilty of something so severe to cause you to not love him, then I'm most certainly not." I joined her at the window. "But what's making you doubt the marriage you've built together? The two of you have been through tough times that have only brought you closer."

"The babies? Or should I say the lack of?"

The loss of life and the inability to have children of their own still shot arrows at her heart … and mine.

"He might be happier with someone else." Allie's voice hardened. "For all I know, maybe he's already considering it … or even acting on it."

She nestled herself deep into the sofa and propped her Birkenstocks on the coffee table. Snowy jumped onto Allie's lap, turned a circle, and then burrowed in a familiar position.

I settled next to my daughter like birds in a nest and eyed my dark brown Air Strides alongside her shoes. "Have you noticed?"

"Noticed what?"

"Neither of our feet look very stylish?" My shoes did look rather wide and … *I swore I'd never become frumpy.*

"These are one of my best-kept secret weapons." She clopped her feet together.

"When I'm angry at Peter, on they go. He hates them—says they look like mini snowshoes strapped on my feet." Allie lifted a foot and tugged on the gray wool sock nestled in the shoe. "Drives him crazy. Says it's a disgrace for the wife of a footwear fashion manager to wear such things."

"Sounds a little passive-aggressive on your end." I continued to eye my shoes, contemplating my love-hate relationship with comfort versus style. "You should tell him what you're angry about."

Allie kicked off both shoes, nestled into the cushions, and crisscrossed her legs. "It's not that easy, Mom. It's not like you and Dad had a perfect relationship. I remember the times he worked late, came home grumpy from a rotten day at the hospital, not even saying hi to you or Reece and me." Allie squeezed a pillow to her chest. "You may not have known it, but I saw you cry while you sat in front of your vanity brushing your hair and fixing your makeup so you'd be pretty when he got home. I even remember your perfume"—she took in a deep breath—"Estee Lauder's Beautiful. You wanted to be beautiful for him, but he didn't notice half the time."

"Your father had a stressful job. Being a surgeon meant long days, hard work." I grabbed a matching pillow and held it to my own chest. "We had a good marriage, even though it probably didn't always look that way."

"He barely talked to you. You stopped going out to dinner, and I swear there were nights after Reece died when I saw you tiptoe down the hall to the guest room." She eyed me suspiciously and continued, "Even though the bed was neatly made when I peeked in the next morning."

"Allie, you're being cruel. Why are you saying all this now?"

"Did you and Dad love each other? Did both of you love … fiercely?" Allie's eyes widened, as if she were hanging on the edge of a precipice and my answer would determine the outcome of her plight.

Fiercely. The word was a saber—able to plunge into my heart or cut the rope that bound my ability to love with abandon ... and forgive, even myself. My response would define everything in my life … past, present, and future. I chose my answer carefully. "Yes."

"How do you know?" Her eyebrows lowered like the narrowing lens of a camera, focusing on my soul.

Was my response sprinkled with seeds of doubt? Did Ray and I love, really love each other all those years, in the happy times as well as the sad?

Envisioning which side the scale would tip—loved or unloved, loving or unloving—I whispered with conviction and truth, "Yes, your dad and I loved each other *fiercely*."

My daughter's eyes softened and she whispered back, "I'm so glad."

As though both of us had been holding our breath underwater, Allie and I exhaled, leaned our heads back, and drew in new breaths—relieved, I believe, that we were still alive.

I pulled back the tab of my soda and offered my aluminum can in a toast. "Here's to true love. Cheers." We clinked cans.

Chapter Seven

Lou ~ Mission Impossible

"Tell me all about your date." Arlene flitted around the kitchen like a fly at a picnic, landing on every appliance and countertop with her industrial-sized bottle of Clorox antibacterial spray.

"My goodness, woman. The house smells like a hospital."

"That's why you pay me the big bucks ... *Joseph.*" With one fluid motion, Arlene lifted the teapot as it whistled, grabbed a cup from the cupboard, filled it with steaming water, and plopped in a tea bag.

"How *do* you do that? More beautiful than that synchronicity swimming."

"*Synchronized* swimming." She swatted my arm with a rag. "And quit trying to change the subject." She joined me at the kitchen table. "Seriously, how did it go? Did Nan, that is her name, right? Did she like El Burrito?"

"Yes, her name is Nan, and she made it clear within the first two minutes to never call her Nancy ... something about an estranged bridge partner."

Before Arlene's tea bag had a chance to surface, she squished it back to its proper place with the tip of a spoon. "Didn't know the game was so emotional."

"You better believe it. I knew a fellow who divorced his wife on the grounds she was a lousy bridge partner."

"No way." Arlene tucked her chin back in such disgust that she appeared to grow a double chin. "How shallow is that?"

"Like a dried-up puddle."

"You got that right." I tracked her movement as she cradled the tea bag in her spoon and airlifted it onto an awaiting saucer. "Back to you."

"Overall, you could say the date was a success."

"That's great news." Arlene beamed as though I had won a prize at a school carnival. "So, you're going out with her again."

"No," I said matter-of-factly. "Nan was definitely better than the health nut who wanted to coach me for an over-eighty marathon. That woman would have put me in the grave. And the one who stood me up for lunch at Viva Dolce was clearly delusional to miss an Italian meal with a full-blooded Italian such as myself."

"But if the date with Nan was a success, then why not see her again?" Her smile deflated. "I don't get you men."

"And we don't get you women." A dollop of sugar plopped into my tea like an exclamation point.

"Shouldn't do that." She raised an eye at my cup. "Not good for you."

"Been putting sugar in my coffee ever since I was a kid. Only time I didn't was during the war shortages or when I was on the front lines." I added another spoonful to make my point.

She pursed her lips in disgust. "If you had a good time, then you should give her another chance. It takes time to know someone."

"Arlene …" The syrupy fluid lingered on my tongue. "Time is what I don't have. I'm eighty-two years old, and when a woman babbles on for half an hour about what a poor choice the restaurant owner made in naming his establishment Small Donkey, the writing is on the wall—this one ain't for me."

"The restaurant's called El Burrrrr-rito, not Small Donkey." Arlene rolled her *r*'s like a pro.

"One and the same. Nan gave me a mini-lesson in Spanish. Said she taught the language in the public schools in Greeley for nearly thirty years. Commendable career." I rubbed my chin, recounting the odd conversation from last night's dinner.

"Then what's her problem with donkeys, especially baby donkeys?" Arlene leaned back and crossed her arms, probably in deep thought as well. "Is a baby donkey a burrito as well, or only small, undersized ones?"

"See what I mean? Now we're having the same crazy discussion I had with Nan. The kicker is she thinks donkeys are filthy animals—stinky, dust-covered, and ornery, so why would anyone in his right mind name an eating establishment after such a beast?"

"Ah, they're cute." When Arlene smiled, years fell from her face. *She really should smile more often.*

"I agree and told her so. That's when our date headed south." For emphasis, I pointed both of my thumbs downward. "To be fair, she kept calling me Joe, and I kept forgetting that was my stage name. She accused me of being rude, ignoring her by not responding."

"What did you tell her?"

"Hard of hearing. Works every time."

"But you said it was a success."

"It was. Delicious guacamole and crispy tamales—the way I like them. As they say, the way to a man's heart is through his stomach." I patted my paunch, a fairly new phenomenon since Betty wasn't around to keep me honest. *Maybe it is time to cut back on the sugar.*

"Liking your meal hardly qualifies for a successful date night."

"Probably true, but going out with Nan confirmed I'm no match for this dating thing. Hank's dare was accepted and attempted, but now it's over. Goodbye to Joseph Marino and ..." I drumrolled the table, and the teacup and saucer clanked in anticipation. "Welcome back, Lou Rizzo."

"You mean lonely Lou." Grabbing the spray bottle and paper towel, Arlene attacked the microwave. "Before you give up, you might want to check the latest notification. Looks like Liaison may have found you the perfect match.

"How in the world do you know that?" My knees popped and cracked as I pushed to a stand—the lovely symphony of old age.

With her head halfway in the microwave, Arlene's giggle was followed by, "I'm the one who helped set up your account."

* * * * *

I'd categorize myself as a dog person, but curiosity killed the cat, and in this case, I was the Cheshire Cat. After Arlene stowed away the vacuum and cleaning bucket in the front closet and blew her customary kiss in my direction, the glowing computer screen beckoned me.

Sly girl. Logging into my profile, then scooting out the door.

Pacing in front of the computer, I contemplated my next move. Turning off the computer would be the easiest. Let the screen turn black and ignore it for a few days. After all, my one-month subscription ended Friday, and I had plenty to occupy my time over the next two days—including lunch with Hank to report on the dare. *He'll get a kick out of the burrito story and can pay me the money he promised.*

A Smith & Sons Hardware calendar teetered by a nail on the wall near my desk. *October.* The pumpkin-laden photo looked pretty much the same each year—pumpkins in a patch, pumpkins in a red wagon, pumpkins on a front porch. The year could have been 2006 as easily as twenty, thirty, forty, or more years ago.

Now empty squares defined my life. Days filled with scribbled notes of kids' birthday parties at crowded pizza parlors, teacher conferences, PTA meetings, dentist appointments, Jennifer's dance recitals, and Brownie Troop meetings. Michael's baseball, driver's education classes, college entrance exams, and application deadlines detailed the busy life of our teenager. Gone.

Michael was about to turn twelve when Jennifer unexpectedly came into our life. Despite the spread of years, they had a deep sister-brother bond—only for a brief seven years before it was broken—shattered and discarded in a remote jungle in Vietnam where my son's lifeless body lay before being flown home to rest in Fort Logan Cemetery.

I hated that year—1969. Even before the year had run its course, I'd torn the calendar from the wall and burned it in the fireplace, watching the paper shrivel and eventually turn to ash as tears streamed down my face.

But then, as life demands, it marched on. Jennifer's birthday parties, dance classes, cheer practice, and tennis matches, along with school dances and orthodontist appointments, took up sole residence as she was the focus of Betty's world and mine. When our only child headed for college, the calendar squares chronicled Betty's aerobic classes, a cooking class here and there, and even a few spotty vacations for us when my work at Fort Carson allowed a break. But still, we missed our daughter's messy room and her nightly phone conversations with pimple-faced boys. Even the stretched-out phone cord in the kitchen drooped listlessly as though it, too, missed her presence.

For a good while, Betty and I limped along. We eventually found a rhythm, moving in unison, going somewhere—a tandem bike of sorts—pointed down a path toward what awaited.

The Army taught me plenty, and one thing was the benefit of efficiency and order—none being wasted in my retirement years. I kept our house in tip-top shape and running like a purring engine. Each New Year's Eve at the stroke of midnight, or earlier as Betty and I aged, the past year's calendar was removed from the wall, tossed in the wastebasket, and replaced with a new, free calendar from old man Smith at the hardware store.

Betty thought it was a bit compulsive to whisk away the past year so readily—without a proper goodbye. She would have preferred to ease into the new year, bask in the memories of the past, and let the passage of time flow into our lives like a calm river.

Again, the calendar stared at me, tidy and void. Even multiple doctor appointments that occupied our days in an effort to banish Betty's cancer had disappeared from the pages of the last two years.

As though to challenge the document of days, I stared down the calendar. Suddenly, I wished I'd boxed up the memories—years and years of events, birthdays, anniversaries—and could bring them back. Gone.

I looked at the computer screen. The glow from that had vanished too. No, all that's in store for me is … memories.

Chapter Eight

Essie ~ Bingo!

Yesterday's conversation with Allie continued to run circles inside my head—our words going nowhere and only adding to the confusion as to what was going on in my daughter's mind. Admittedly, my mind became clouded in the process. *Do I know any longer what real love is?*

Maybe admitting my shoes were frumpy or something more ethereal, but my hand joggled the mouse, awakening the computer. With the month-long subscription ending in two days, I could let Allie's silly idea dissipate like fog and accept being alone. Lonely? Loveless? The semantics didn't matter. I'd survived worse in my life. *No, I refuse to own either of those words … not only for myself but also for Allie. A mother is never too old to breathe hope into her child's life.*

The computer awakened with a whir and a chug. Was it pleasantly surprised to see me, or preferred to remain in the slumber assumed after Ray passed? He was the one who believed it important to keep up, or at least shuffle behind technology. *Essie, it's imperative we old folk keep up with the times to keep us young.* His mantra played in my mind, but even his conviction to remain modernized couldn't keep the passage of time from wreaking havoc on his health.

Now, approximately every ninth week—depending on the losses and gains to the Golden Girls group—it was my turn to host the gathering from church, and I could count on a comment or two about the sleek Apple computer on the kitchen console.

Well before I earned membership, the group had been coined the Double Gs among the other social circles at the Evergreen Community Church. To me, the nickname sounded like an outrageous bra size, indicative of a bunch of old women with saggy breasts sitting around lamenting their losses, the low ratio of eligible men to women, and their latest health issues.

But I'd grown fond of the women, and despite none of us ever wishing to qualify for membership, we found ourselves in a shared situation. The blank stares I'd received at the last meeting indicated the ladies didn't appreciate the analogy I'd shared. I likened us to the last of autumn's ripened apples, dangling together from the same branch as we lived out our days, not sure when or who would be the next to drop. To me, it was quite poetic, all of us in the same season of life.

So as Liaison's intertwined heart logo filled the screen, GG comments echoed in my mind, "Be careful of those *viruses* on the Internet—no telling what you might catch," or "Gee, Essie, you must spend a fortune shopping online." And my friend Ginny's constant lament, "I wish my grandson would teach me how to use one of those so I could be in touch with the *real* world."

Ignoring their voices playing tug-of-war in my mind—and perhaps against my own better judgment—I peeked into my account a final time. Could someone successfully shop online for love?

Joseph. Age eighty-two. Nice enough looking. Hair. Actually, quite a bit. Wonder if he goes by Joe?

"Hmm? Colonel, US Army, Retired. Impressive," I muttered and scanned his lengthy About Me profile. "Either he thinks quite highly of himself, or he's potentially interesting." Situating my reading glasses, I leaned toward the screen. "Okay, Joe. I'm giving you two minutes to convince me you're worth my time."

* * * * *

"He's passionate about Italian food." My hands were busy folding dishtowels as I waited for Allie's response over my cell-phone speaker. "And his country."

"Italy?" Allie's voice was flat. "Age?"

"No. He's passionate about the United States. He was a colonel in the Army." For a moment, it felt like the return of a dreaded hot flash from my fifties. "And he's eighty-two." Instead, my daughter's interrogation had me under a spotlight.

"He's old."

"So am I."

"Married?"

"Of course not! Why would he be on Liaison?"

"Plenty of creeps out there, Mom."

"He's a widower … and he looks nice enough."

Joe's small photo gallery was displayed on the screen like an amateur scrapbooker's page. What must have been a recent portrait of him in uniform confirmed he was a proud veteran, and for a moment, I caught myself imagining how handsome he must have been as a young soldier. In another photo, he stood on the observation tower of the Empire State Building with his arm wrapped around an attractive woman. There was a striking resemblance—perhaps his daughter—with soft brown eyes, high cheekbones, a head of thick hair, and a wide smile. The third picture was probably taken in his home where he reclined in a large leather chair wearing full Denver Bronco attire—blue-and-orange sweatshirt and matching hat.

"He likes football," I added.

"But you don't."

"Never said that. I just wouldn't plop on a couch and watch it all day." Admittedly, Joe appeared ecstatic wearing the football garb—a potential cause for concern. "At least he didn't paint his face, and he's definitely not that Barrel Man who's half-naked and cheering on national television."

"Gee, that makes me feel a little better."

"Allie, are you upset about this match?" I stuffed the towels into the already full drawer. "Remember this was your idea to begin with."

"And I'm the one who's supposed to be doing the communicating and getting to know a person first before they meet the real you. No weirdos make it past the initial inquiry since I screen them thoroughly."

"That's appreciated, dear. But I'm capable of discerning whether someone is, as you say, a creep or not. After all, I've made it through life this far, and your father wasn't a weirdo."

"He's the only man you were ever with. Fifty-six years with the same person didn't allow you many dating mishaps."

"Don't you think for a minute I was a prude. Plenty of other young men were interested in me before your dad and I married."

A long exhale over the phone followed. "At least let me go into your account and take a look at this *Joe*. Give me today to respond to him, see if he's interested in writing back. That way, I can get a better feel of who he is before we decide if this match should go any further."

It drove me crazy when the kids used to tell little fibs. Now I wondered if my nose had grown like Pinocchio's in the worn picture book I had read to my young children, hoping to distill virtue. As I touched my nose, another vintage memory surfaced. I was standing in the kitchen, the black-and-white tiled floor slick beneath my stocking feet. I had slipped off my shoes at the back door—didn't want to be caught sneaking handfuls of the freshly baked cookies intended for the new neighbors. My plan was foiled when the spatula tumbled off the counter, clanging onto the floor. Mother had charged into the kitchen, her face as red as the rickrack sewn on the hem of her apron. Caught. I pleaded it was all my older brother, Edward's, idea. Mother sternly reminded me he wasn't home yet from school. Caught again. Sent to bed early and without dinner—disgraced for my dishonesty.

I had to come clean with Allie. "Joe's asked me to meet him for coffee ... and I accepted."

Silence.

"At the Coffee Bean Bistro on Main. Ten-thirty in the morning." There, I was honest. No need to feel guilty. "He lives in Golden. Couldn't believe he's in a neighboring town."

Allie's voice was soft and her words measured. "Are you *sure*? I mean, do you feel comfortable meeting him by yourself? Maybe I should go with you."

"Of course I'm nervous. But it's only coffee ... in the daytime."

"You don't like coffee."

"Coffee. Tea. I'm sure they serve both. Besides, what's the worst that can happen? We meet, a sudden appointment has come up for my bad case of bunions, and I limp out the door."

"Good thinking." Allie giggled, breaking the tension as though a taut rubber band strung along our communication line had finally snapped. "I'm sure you'll be fine. At least you don't have to hop on a plane to have dinner with him if things work out ... and stay with the name Esther. Keep things super formal until we know more about him."

Thoughts dangled between us, replaced only with mutual sighs.

"Thank you for wanting to take such good care of me," I said.

"That's what daughters are supposed to do." The sound of Allie's smacking lips swept through the phone and landed on my cheek. "We make a good team ... even if you fired your ghostwriter."

Chapter Nine

Essie~ Coffee for Two

Encouraging was not the word that came to mind when I paused at my reflection in the coffee shop window. *Shouldn't have worn a skirt—too dressy. Brown sweater—drab. At least the scarf is colorful ... and will hide the hives should my nerves get the best of me. Haven't had those in years.*

"You can do this, Essie," I whispered, opening the door and stepping inside to the mixed aroma of coffee and cinnamon rolls.

Acoustic music played from an invisible speaker, gurgling under the conversations at the tables like a soothing stream. Two young mothers sipped their drinks—most likely their caffeine-infused lifelines after sleep-deprived nights. One had a baby snuggled under a swath of cloth wrapped neatly across her chest. Peeking eyes, a button nose, and downy hair poked from the top of the fabric like a joey nestled with its mama kangaroo. The other baby slept in a stroller—those precious moments when the mother could relax. Five suited men crowded around a four-seat table, elbows on the table and brows furrowed—perhaps big conference-room talk around a too-small table.

A young man with Mickey Mouse sized headphones occupied a corner spot, most likely a student at the local community college in good company with a stack of textbooks, an open laptop, a giant cup of coffee, and a bagel with cream cheese.

The establishment was cozy, and it didn't take more looking to consider the possibility Joe might stand me up. My watch read twenty-five minutes after ten. *Early. I didn't plan on that, and I surely don't want to appear overly anxious to meet him.*

A vacant table waited next to the west window. Sunny and warm, not too loud and away from the other patrons, but not so isolated that I couldn't call for help if he turned out to be, as Allie said, a creep.

I chose the chair facing the entrance, and for a moment, felt a slight panic at the notion that I might not recognize him from his profile picture. *Silver hair, nice smile, old guy ... oh, my ... what did he anticipate about my appearance?* I fluffed my scarf around my neck, already feeling the heat and ensuing red blotches resurfacing from my teenage days. I rummaged in my purse for a piece of paper and pen and began to write a new grocery and to-do list—anything to distract me and calm my pounding heart.

Prescription drop-off. Order new checks. November's Bunco sign-up. Library for book club novel. Oatmeal. Cottage cheese. Tums. Toilet paper. Bananas. Strawberries. Broccoli ...

"Esther?"

The voice pulled me from the produce aisle, and I glanced up.

"I'm Joe." He flashed the same full smile from his photograph and then offered his hand. "Only a portion of my name, rank, and serial number. You know those online rules."

"Es ... Esther." I shook his hand. *No need to divulge too much either. Stick with Allie's plan.*

"Looks like you're intent on writing that list."

I fumbled with the slip of paper and pen and tucked them into my purse. "A bit of organizing. I'm a list-maker. Don't like to forget things." *Oh, that was dumb. He'll think I'm senile.* I cringed, hoping he hadn't been standing next to me for long. *Tums. Toilet paper. Really?*

"May I join you?" He gestured toward the empty chair.

"Please." I folded my hands on my lap, acutely aware of the butterflies in my stomach. As he settled into the chair, the sun captured the pleasing green-and-brown mixture of his eye color. *Mostly brown. Nice.*

"Thanks for accepting my offer for coffee, Esther with no last name." He grinned, producing deep dimples alongside wrinkles that come with happy and sad times.

He wore a gray-and-white checked button-down shirt and a light gray sweater with a slight collar and zipper. Straight, white teeth—*must have had them done.* Handsome—not wearing many of the typical badges of old age. *In fact, he's a shiny silver dollar.*

"That's a nice-looking scarf you have on there."

Had he read my mind and felt obligated to return a compliment?

"Thank you." I fumbled with the knot. "Autumn colors—my favorite season. You?"

"Colors? Or favorite season?"

"Both, I suppose."

"Hard to beat the fall in Colorado. Perfect weather, and I never tire of watching the aspen trees change colors." He looked out the window. "They're already glowing."

"One of my favorite drives is over Independence Pass, but I haven't been up there in years."

"I haven't either. Spectacular scene ... but you'd better keep one eye on the road."

"Especially the way those RVs swing around the curves—nearly pushing you off the cliffs." *Don't sound like such a ninny.*

"But the view's worth the danger, don't you think?" He revealed a boyish grin that must have served him well. Probably stole plenty of hearts in his earlier days.

"Absolutely. Those RVs are overrated. I've always preferred tent camping."

There, I redeemed myself.

"Agreed. Nothing like snuggling in a sleeping bag and waking up to the quiet of a tent." He smiled. "But as I got older, didn't think I'd care much for the winters—maybe head south to Arizona with the snowbirds, but I never fell for that." He folded his hands on the table, and like my own, his were unable to hide the passing of the years. Paper-thin skin pulled tightly over enlarged knuckles, adjoined to wrinkled and spotted areas above the thumb and top of his hands. Veins protruded, coursing like life's many journeys.

He must have noticed my stare. He slipped his hands apart, revealing what remained of his thumb and forefinger on his left hand. "Lost part of it in the second war." He wriggled a stump, cut short just below the joint. "Lucky for me, that's all I left in the Philippines."

"I'm sorry."

He gave me a quizzical look.

"I mean for your hand."

He slid his hands from the table, perhaps stowing away his war stories for another day. We sat in silence for a moment like perennials waiting for the right time to sprout.

I was about to thank him for his service, as that seemed the right thing to do. But, before I could speak, he suddenly crossed his hands on his chest, and I wondered if he was having a heart attack.

"I almost forgot. I have something for you." He unzipped his sweater and retrieved a single red rose wrapped in plastic. He removed the protective covering and held the beautiful rose out to me. "*Ciao bella*. A rose for a beautiful lady … my apologies it wilted."

"It's beautiful. How thoughtful … and like magic," I whispered, "it appeared from nowhere."

"From my heart." He patted his chest. "I'm old-school … from the days when a man presented a lady with flowers."

A cool breeze blew through the partially open window, but my face felt warm—bathed in the pleasant sensation of a man's attention and, at the same time, the awkwardness of accepting a compliment from a stranger. *Stranger? Somehow our meeting doesn't seem strange.*

"How about a coffee? Actually, I'm more of a tea drinker." I gestured to the elaborate chalkboard menu above the register. It may as well have been Einstein's handwritten theory of relativity as the choices, items, and descriptions were far from a cup of black coffee or tea with a splash of cream.

"How rude of me." He pushed himself from the table.

He cocked his head toward the girl behind the counter, who was busy twirling her purple strands of hair around her forefinger and reading the inscription on her coworker's tattooed bicep.

He touched my forearm. "What would you like to drink? And how about a pastry? Those cinnamon rolls have caught my eye." He winked. "As have you."

Then he laughed—a beautiful sound that stirred my heart and confirmed I wasn't too old to get butterflies in my stomach.

Chapter Ten

Lou ~ Reporting In

In his customary manner, Hank slurped his spaghetti. As if a hotheaded woman had slapped his face, the last whip of the noodle left a splotch of red sauce on his chin.

"Napkin." Our code word for *you've got food on your face* rolled off my lips like we'd performed the duet a thousand times. "How's the square dancing treating you and Libby? Do you wear those matching outfits?"

"She'd be awfully happy if I would. Gingham just isn't my style."

I raised my eyebrows. "Good to know."

"Besides, we're taking a break from the dancing. Said her ingrown toenail is acting up."

"The two of you share that kind of information?" Feigning to hide my disgust, I wiped my mouth with my paper napkin.

"Why not? We're pretty close these days." He leaned back in his chair and stretched his lanky arms over his head. "Even talking about marriage."

My reaction would have been smoother if I had covered my entire head with the chintzy serviette. Instead, my lower jaw may as well have hit the edge of the table.

"Why are you so surprised?" Hank's response was so casual one would have thought he mentioned it might rain later today. "She's a wonderful woman—kind, honest, thinks I'm funny and smart." He made a check mark in the air. "Good enough tally for me."

"How old is she? Younger than you, I'm sure."

"Nine years, but who's counting when you're this far over the hill.

Seventies. Eighties. All relative depending on how you want to live your life." He leaned forward, elbows on the table, and locked eyes with mine.

I braced myself for his interrogation, which to this point in our lunch hadn't occurred.

"Tell me about it. Time to report into your old buddy."

"About what?" Busying myself with swiping breadcrumbs into a neat pile would buy me only a few moments.

"You know exactly what I'm talking about. That's part of the deal."

"Tell you about my date like you're my mother? Besides, it was a dare. I didn't make a deal with you … except you still owe me the money."

"For what?" Hank scrunched his face so hard he looked like a dried-out raisin.

"Doesn't matter." I waved him off. "We actually had a great time." An image of Esther's pretty face sneaked into my mind. "She's quite a looker. I never would've guessed she's eighty—figured early seventies at the most."

"Is that right?"

"White hair, the good-looking kind that's attractive. Nicely dressed. Classy."

"And?" Hank prodded.

"On the short side, but not wide. Just right, I'd say. Walks faster than me. I had to step it up a notch to keep up with her in the parking lot."

"Sounds promising." Hank puckered his lips as if calculating my responses. "Any plans beyond a coffee date? Maybe lunch?"

The wine was smooth and slid down my throat before I answered. "Already have."

"Asked her out again?"

"No. Already had lunch." I drank again, enjoying watching my friend's curiosity pique. "Right after we had coffee … decided we were hungry and still had more to talk about. We extended our date down the street to Maggie's Deli and Dine.

"Isn't that something?" Hank shook his head. "You the talker."

"She's interesting. Funny too. She makes me laugh." I grinned at the thought of Esther's warm smile. "Haven't been doing much of that the last few years. Feels good."

"Will you see her again?"

"Tomorrow evening."

"For dinner."

"She's making the meal at her home."

"Lou Rizzo, I underestimated you." Hank extended his hand across the table. "Congratulations, Casanova."

"Thanks, but how do I tell her I'm not Joseph Marino?"

* * * * *

Reporting to Arlene wasn't as easy as with Hank. I'd been around long enough to know females have a different way of assessing the success or failure of a date.

"What did you talk about?" Arlene smacked her gum as she faced me across the kitchen table. "Tell me all the details."

"Can't remember. We talked about all sorts of things." I creased the morning's paper and pretended to read. "And I know you left your vacuum here on purpose—sneaky, considering you cleaned last week."

"I was in the neighborhood—convenient to swing by and pick it up." She blew a small bubble, then popped it in the corner of her mouth.

"You should avoid that, especially if you're on a date." I adjusted my reading glasses and focused on the newsprint.

"So now you're a dating expert?"

I ignored her question.

"Seriously. Fill me in, *Joseph.*"

Her emphasis on my pseudonym clonked me over the head. Maybe Arlene's mid-morning flyby was a blessing in disguise. She'd know how to get me out of this snarc. Hank didn't have a clue, only suggested I tell Esther mild dementia caused me to occasionally forget my name.

"We're having dinner tonight at her house." The first information leak.

"Fabulous!" Arlene's face lit up as if I'd won the lottery. "I had a good feeling about this one."

"I'll admit, I'm a little excited about Esther. She's fun to be around— light, but not ditzy or boring. Smart too. We talked about what's going on in the world. I like that in a woman, solid foot in the door with current events." My index finger tapped the newspaper. "We even shared some about our religious beliefs."

Arlene propped her chin on folded hands, clearly waiting for more.

"Told her I was brought up Catholic, and Betty and I raised the kids in the church. She's Protestant, but mainly says she's nondenominational— goes to Evergreen Community Church."

"You shared about your wife?"

49

"Only a little. Told her we'd been married fifty-eight years before Betty passed. Esther was with her husband … can't remember his name right now, fifty-six. He died about two years ago as well, six months before Betty." I ran my fingers along the rim of the china teacup, the ones Betty inherited from her Aunt Mabel and insisted we use instead of cheap ceramic mugs. *Life is brief, so why not use what is precious.* My wife's words seeped into my mind as they often did in my dreams. "Hearts are precious, but fragile, aren't they?"

Except for the incessant beeping of the message machine, announcing someone most likely wanted to sell me something, silence hovered between Arlene and me—allowing our private thoughts to ebb and flow as currents in a slow-moving stream.

Then, like a pebble tossed in the water, Arlene's voice broke the fluidity of my memories. "Is she from around here?"

"Raised here in Golden. She and her husband moved up to Evergreen when they had children. Figured it was close enough to his medical practice in the city but better to raise their kids in a smaller town. Even though she's two years younger than me … I wonder if we could have been at the same high school at some point.

"You should look in your old yearbook, see if she's in there. Do you still have that around?"

"Heavens no, not with moving the way we did when I was in the service. Can't remember if I ever had the book. Besides, I only attended Golden High half my senior year. Big school. Didn't know many people—pretty much kept to myself." *Especially after the accident.* I pushed myself from the table, a sudden need to excuse myself.

"You all right? You're pale." Arlene stood.

"I'm fine." I set off toward the bathroom—no need to share the past.

Once the door was closed and locked, I was able to breathe. For years, I'd willed away the memory from consuming fitful dreams. Now, it sneaked in, even in the daylight, like a bold intruder. The accident happened so long ago, well before the nightmares of the wars that were well deserving of heart palpitations, hot sweats, and insomnia.

Instead, nearly sixty-five years ago, my determination to be first down a sledding hill, and the result of that decision, drilled a hole in my heart that never healed. Forever, my penance was sealed—slowly and painfully tortured as each granule of sand slipped through the passage of time, a reoccurring reminder of the horrific outcome of my actions.

After a fake flush and running the basin water, I returned to the kitchen.

"You okay?" The narrowing of Arlene's eyes showed her genuine concern.

She's a good friend. "Good to go now. Stomach's a little upset, that's all."

"You should take a nap—rest up before your dinner with Esther."

"Maybe I should cancel." I feigned a yawn.

"Only if you think you're coming down with something. Otherwise, you should keep a good thing going—keep it on a roll if you know what I mean." Arlene pursed her lips. "But I'm curious. If you intend to see her again, how are you going to tell her your real name?"

"Good question. What's your advice?"

"Be honest. Tell her the truth about wanting to ease into the online dating—flying under the radar. You're an Army guy. She'll understand the strategy."

"That would be Air Force."

She puffed her lips and looked me square in the eyes as only a person could who's been toughened by life. "You're a good man, Lou. Don't be afraid to let her know who you really are."

And ... admit to myself who I am?

Chapter Eleven

Essie ~ Do Tell

Phyllis' voice bubbled through the phone like champagne. "Ginny and I want you to come with us to tonight's *Be a Star with Starry Night* at Party and Paint. It's a Van Gogh theme, and we love those Frenchmen … or was he Dutch? Oh well. Doesn't matter. We just want to have a fun girls' night and can pick you up at six-thirty."

"Thanks for thinking of me. I wish I could. Try me again next month." I grabbed a dishcloth and wiped the kitchen counter a third time, a not-so-subtle attempt to erase my fib.

Phyllis' invitation was tempting, if only to laugh with my girlfriends. They knew I loved art—visiting museums and exhibits, catching the latest artsy flick about a tormented, but genius artist at the Chez Artiste theater. They even complimented me on the florals and landscapes hanging in various rooms in my home—all with my signature. But, for reasons my friends would never understand and I would never share, those pieces were created before Reece died. I'd buried my brushes in the closet along with my past.

In high school, with my art teacher's encouragement, I entertained the thought of attending a fine art school. Whether I'd become a success or the proverbial starving artist didn't matter, he said. "Esther," he insisted, "you have a gift, and you should do something with it."

Then the reality of World War II hung over the country like a black cloud, and anything that hinted of frivolity was replaced with sensible pursuits. Becoming a nurse seemed the right thing to do according to my parents and my conscience.

My painting supplies were packed away, ignored through college and early marriage. How easily the pleasure derived from creating something from a blank canvas was forgotten—something I couldn't buy at a store or satisfy with other hobbies and pursuits.

Later, when Ray continued to work long hours at the hospital and I cut back my nursing hours to be home with the kids, I rendezvoused with paints and brushes, late at night and early in the morning when the house was quiet. Like reacquainting with a childhood best friend, we seamlessly picked up where we'd left off.

But then the accident happened, and the joy of painting slipped away, as if it could no longer meet me in such a blissful place. Instead, it wandered off in search of a new soul to fulfill—a soul deserving of such pleasure.

My thoughts bounced back to Phyllis. She was talking about someone and somewhere … or something like that. "One of these times, I'll join you." *Another lie.* "I haven't painted for so long I'd surely disgrace poor old Vincent." *Truth.*

"Oh, he won't care a bit." Phyllis' laugh was contagious and I giggled. "Well, next month is Harvest with Henri, and I hear he's a hoot." She paused. "Hey, I bet you're seeing that man you met online again tonight, aren't you?"

"I am."

"Ginny filled me in, but I want to hear all the details from the horse's mouth. Coffee followed with lunch, all in one day." Phyllis clicked her tongue as if I'd done something naughty. "Is that considered a double date?"

"That would be two couples, Phyllis, four people."

"Then it was a double-decker date." A shrill whistle followed. "You must have really impressed him. He's taking you out again, a few days after you first met?"

"Actually, I'm having him over to my house for dinner … Phyllis, are you there?"

"Yes. Only thinking that the third time is a charm. Isn't that what they say?"

Now it was my turn to be silent. Could a person have a second chance at love? "We'll see, my friend. I'll let you know how the evening plays out."

We said our goodbyes and hung up. With a couple of steps toward the bathroom to shower and do my make-up, the phone sounded again. I considered letting it go to voicemail, but the caller ID read Allie

LaFleur. *You only get a minute.*

"Hey, Mom." Allie sounded deflated. "Do you have a minute? What time is your big date?"

An element of sarcasm dropped into her last two words like a teaspoon of vinegar. "In an hour. I still have to shower and finish the salad. What do you need, dear?"

"Nothing that can't wait."

"For heaven's sake, I know you better than that."

"Okay." A heavy sigh seemed to weigh down the phone. "I asked Peter if he is seeing another woman. It was more like a confrontation."

"And? What did he say?"

"He said I was completely crazy. That he loves me and is committed to our marriage one-hundred percent."

"Do you believe him?"

"I think so ... of course, I want to."

"The two of you need special time together. Any chance you could take a vacation? I can stop in and feed Snowy, or she can stay here."

"That's probably a good idea, especially before I start another manuscript and get accused of carousing with another man."

"Good thinking."

"I'll ask Peter if he can take the time off. Maybe I'll surprise him and book a stay somewhere in the mountains. Vail is always romantic. We can pretend we're strolling through Switzerland or Austria—somewhere exotic. Well, that's not exactly exotic, but you know what I mean."

"Fairy-tale-like."

"That's it," her voice perked an octave. "If Snowy could stay with you, that would help. She's been mopey lately. Maybe she needs a Prince Charming."

"Please wait on the matchmaking until you and Peter are home to supervise." The kitchen clock reminded me the days were long gone when I could run a brush through my hair, swipe on some lipstick, and be ready to go. "Honey, I have to go. Let's talk tomorrow."

"Love you, Mom. Have fun tonight."

"I plan to. I hope he likes—"

"Everything wonderful about you."

"Thanks, honey."

"Daddy would be happy to know Joseph makes you laugh."

"He would, wouldn't he?"

"By the way, Rose Petal Pink lipstick is a good color on you."

"Thanks for the tip."

"*Bon chance*. Luck of the Irish." A girlish giggle followed, reminding me that even hopeless romantics like my daughter had a sense of humor tucked within bouquets of flowers. "And since he's Italian, *buona fortuna*."

"You're ridiculous, but whatever it is, I may need it. Now, goodnight."

The phone clicked off and I set it to Silent. No more interruptions—I had serious work to do.

Chapter Twelve

Essie ~ Dinner and Details

Another lap around the dining table was beginning to feel like a track meet at the local high school. I eyed the table a last time. Adding one leaf would have been better—maybe it's too small and intimate. No, that would be odd to sit at opposite ends and shout at one another as if we needed hearing aids. *I don't think he wears them, does he?* I hadn't noticed, but then again, we had a lot to learn about each other.

The knife and fork at one place setting received a final straightening, and the napkin at the other was refolded a third time. I considered lighting the candles, but Joseph was fifteen minutes late. They'd be gloppy stubs by the time dinner was served, especially if he didn't come at all.

My feet already throbbed from the black pumps pulled from the rear of my closet. Clearly, they were a better choice from a style vantage point—a nice pairing with my black slacks and turquoise blouse. Small matching earrings and a pendant from a trip to Santa Fe completed my outfit. Turquoise—that unique, unearthed stone, gifted on special occasions from Ray, had a way of making me feel grounded and confident. Tonight, I needed both. The doorbell rang and I jumped. *So much for being calm.*

"Good evening, Esther." A stunning bouquet of sunflowers, lilies, and lavender preceded Joseph into the foyer. "Forgive me for being late. I tried to call."

"Oh, that's my mistake. My phone was silenced."

"Still my fault. I underestimated the line at the floral shop. Must be a big night for us young boys heading out on dates." He kissed my hand.

"Completely out of character for me to be tardy. Learned in the military to be prompt. In fact, fifteen minutes early is on time." He handed me the flowers and set his jacket on the foyer bench.

"You're fine, and the flowers are beautiful. Feeling a little weak in the knees, I carried the bouquet into the kitchen. After arranging the flowers in a vase of water, I placed them in the center of the dining room table. "There, we can enjoy them during dinner."

"Good. Then the flowers were worth the wait."

"And so are you." I smiled, relieved he hadn't changed his mind about tonight.

"You look lovely. Your hair is so pretty."

Instinctively, my hand went to my temple and smoothed my hair. "Why, thank you. It was quite dark when I was younger. I followed after my mother. Her hair skipped the gray and went straight to white."

"Pure white, just like salt," he added. "You are stunning tonight, my dear Salt."

"Hmm? Never been called that nickname." I reached up and tentatively touched his hair, neatly trimmed above the ear. It felt soft and downy—a foreign sensation to touch another man in an innocent, yet intimate way. Quickly, I pulled my hand away and fumbled with my necklace. "And even though your hair leans toward silver, I think I'll call you Pepper."

His coordinating, silver-haired brows raised.

"Because you *pepper* me with compliments." I smiled.

"Then I'd say we make a good pair."

Like awkward teenagers, both of us shifted our weight, and I was sure his face turned a shade of pink.

Joseph spared us further embarrassment. "Well, I'm looking forward to our evening ... and the meal. Smells delicious. Italian cuisine woos my heart every time."

* * * * *

Cheese and wine evoke good conversation, and my choices from Sam's Gourmet must have aged well. After enjoying appetizers in the front room, we transitioned to the dining room, where, at one point, Joseph reached across the table and held my hand.

Shared passions became apparent, and individual likes seemed to pique our interest in each other as our talk flowed throughout the evening like a calm river —peaceful, refreshing, and headed somewhere full of life.

Our pasts flitted into the conversations from time to time, but only to remind us of our shared place in life—histories rich in love of country, family, and even faith, though that was a topic I noticed Joseph chose not to dwell on too long or deep.

I think we both found it rejuvenating not to reminisce at length, but instead open our eyes to the person sitting across the table—a person still worthy of listening ears and an encouraging smile.

Clearly, Joseph's years of military service, spanning World War II, Korea, and Vietnam had shaped him into the patriotic, proud, and worldly man he'd become. From the three times we'd shared company in only one week, he was the perfect gentleman—his morals, ethics, and values chiseled deeply into his core.

"So, you enjoy your church group," he said.

"They're a sweet group of ladies. Often we laugh, sometimes we cry. Lonely, most of them. But we provide each other fellowship and help keep the focus on what really matters."

"Are you lonely, Esther?"

I paused, allowing myself to answer honestly. "In some ways, yes. Ray and I were married for so many years, just like you and your wife. But we were independent too. I was always busy. Probably too busy."

"We're similar in that way."

"How so?"

"My career mostly. The military kept me away a lot. Shortly after Betty and I married, I was off to Japan, Saudi Arabia, Italy, Korea, and, finally, Germany. The family joined me during some of those periods, but I was working hard—moving up the military ranks and doing my patriotic duty. My wife raised the two kids. Then we lost Michael in Vietnam." Sadness darkened his face as though the curtain fell at the end of a Shakespearean tragedy.

"You mentioned that at lunch. I'm so sorry." I sipped my wine, attempting to push away my own loss of a son. "My brother died at a young age, but I can't imagine losing your own child."

My words slapped me across my face. I had openly denied the existence of my son. I grabbed Joseph's hand and dug my fingers into his skin.

His eyes grew wide as if he, too, had been struck.

"Oh God. I'm a horrible person." I slumped back in my chair, self-defeated.

His questioning eyes demanded an explanation, but his kind voice calmed the unexpected storm that raged in me. "Talk to me, Esther."

"It's true I had a brother who died, but ... Ray and I had a son ... Reece." Saying his name stabbed at my heart. "He was killed in a car accident shortly before he turned twenty." I bowed my head. "I have no idea why I said what I did. You must think I'm crazy ... or a monster for denying my own child's existence."

"You're not a monster. Our minds act unexpectedly ... especially when something from the past continues to haunt us. Your heart, mine too, still aches from losing a son, especially much too early."

Joseph took my hands in his and held them gently, rubbing his thumb on mine. Ray used to do the same, especially after Reece died, holding my hand when we lay in bed together, waiting for sleep that wouldn't come.

* * * * *

Perhaps it was the wine, but for the remainder of the meal, we enjoyed a lighter atmosphere. Joseph talked about tracking his Italian genealogy, consuming beefy, fact-filled history books, and described some of his favorite places to take brisk walks along the Highline Canal. He raised his arm and flexed his bicep. Though his dress shirt hid proof of his brawn, his mind and body were obviously a duo that served him well. When he wasn't out with his buddy, Hank, or at a veteran's affair, he spent time online, playing competitive Solitaire—which I said was an oxymoron. He agreed but confessed he was too addicted to give it up.

After we finished too much food—rigatoni with meatballs and my specialty, eggplant Parmesan—only because I couldn't decide which to make and which he would prefer, Joseph convinced me to tell him about my paintings displayed in the living room. I believe he was sincere when he pointed out my talent, especially for creating landscapes.

"Maybe I could commission you to paint a piece for me. Consider a fair price and let's talk ... an original Esther White to grace my home." He surveyed a large painting of a field of poppies against a backdrop of cypress trees. "Reminds me of my ancestral home. Italy ... a breathtaking slice of the planet."

The mention of me painting again caught me off guard, and I changed the subject. "I'd love to see it someday. Ray and I talked about going to Europe, but it never happened."

"Perhaps it's not too late. After all, la *vita 'e un vaggio* ... life is a journey."

"And to that, I agree."

"Hey, I have a great idea. Let's take a selfie in front of the painting. We'll pretend we jetted off to Tuscany." He pulled his cell phone from his pocket.

We laughed as he tried to position the phone for a selfie. Our first attempts resulted in lopsided photos of the opposite living room wall, then we discovered the reverse camera icon. With faces cheek-to-cheek within the tiny photo frame, we got the giggles. Felt wonderful to laugh until my belly hurt—in a good way.

Realizing the photo session wasn't going to end well, I motioned him away from the painting and back to the sofa area for more good conversation … *and more lessons in Italian.*

We were enjoying store-bought tiramisu in the family room when I got a wild hair to retrieve something from the basement.

"Sit tight. I'll be right back with a surprise." Worried I'd catch a heel on the carpeted stairs, I slipped off my shoes and descended into the storage room. When I emerged, Joseph had slipped his shoes off as well—a good indication he wasn't in a hurry to leave.

I settled on the sofa next to him a little closer than I'd expected my derriere to land. To help cover the awkward transition, I plopped the faded book on our shared laps.

"Oh my." He bent closer and read the inscription, "Golden High School, 1941."

"I wonder if we were ever in the same circles. Maybe we'll remember seeing each other, even though I must have been a sophomore when you were a senior."

Joseph shifted his weight, jostling the book as though he was suddenly uncomfortable. "You won't find me in there. My family left New York in November and arrived in Colorado well after the school year had begun."

"Maybe not your formal portrait, but let's see if you're in a candid or maybe a team photo. Did you play any sports? Join the debate team or anything like that?"

"None I can remember."

His demeanor was noticeably different. Perhaps he wasn't too fond of his school memories or the fact he'd been uprooted in his senior year. I tried to make light of the change in mood. "Whatever you did, I bet you were impressive." I flipped to the senior class section and ran my fingers down the alphabetical listing. "That's a shame. No Joseph Marino recorded here."

"Then let's not continue the scavenger hunt for me." He shifted the book onto his lap. "What was your maiden name?"

"Owens. I'd be under Esther Owens."

The dessert was overly rich, but I was stunned when Joseph coughed, pushed the yearbook onto the coffee table, and lurched from the sofa.

"My goodness, are you all right?" I stood and took him by the arm. "You're shaking."

He cleared his throat and then waved me off, hastier than expected. "You'll have to excuse me … this darn stomach is acting up. Had some trouble earlier today, should have known better and canceled tonight." He started for the front door.

"Are you okay to drive? I can take you home." I hurried after him, stopping to retrieve his jacket from the bench.

"Essie, I really have to go. I'm sorry …*mi dispiace*." Again, he waved me off, disappeared out the front door, and drove away.

After slowly closing the door, I wandered back through the dining room, noting the remnants of what I thought was a lovely meal. Next, in the living room, I reached to switch off the end-table lamp—a fitting response to a bizarre ending to the night. But before I darkened the room, I stopped and stared at the painting of the vibrant orange and crimson fields of poppies. *What in the world happened to a beginning that seemed so right, so full of promise?*

Chapter Thirteen

Lou ~ Duck and Cover

"Fool!" I slammed the medicine cabinet, jostling my reflection like the nerves that wracked my body.

At the mention of her maiden name, I knew exactly who she was. Essie Owens, the younger sister of Edward Owens. *Beloved son of Jonathon and Faye Owens.* The obituary hadn't faded from my mind, not like the tangible paper it was printed on sixty-four years ago, long since disintegrated in the fireplace when I tried to extinguish the memory.

The moment the yearbook surfaced, the possibility of a relationship between Essie and me was over. No possibility of moving forward when the past proved once again to be my ball and chain. Like Dickens' Jacob Marley, my past decisions would haunt me for eternity.

Before flicking off the light, I considered calling Esther to apologize again for my hasty exit. My sudden stomachache had been convincing, so much so that she helped rummage for my keys in my jacket pocket. Poor woman. She's probably worried. I assured her it wasn't the meal—after all, I'd told her the pain acted up earlier, and I should have had the sense to cancel our date. Now, my anxiety was turning me into a pathological liar as well.

I'll call her tomorrow. Explain that the dating life wouldn't work out for an old guy like me. *She deserves better anyway.*

Before setting my phone on the nightstand, I pulled up the photo we'd taken earlier in the evening.

How strange. Her beautiful face and smile are captured in my phone. Looking at her warmed my heart, fanning the desire to know her better. Before my thoughts were wrangled, I imagined kissing her. *You ole sap.*

You act like you have feelings for her.

I turned off the light and stared into the darkness. "I don't deserve to love again." The statement—spoken aloud—startled me. Alone, the only audible reply was the ticking clock on the wall. Time had no intention of stopping—or for that matter, erasing the past from which it came.

The electric blanket failed to keep me warm even as I pulled it closer to my chin. After lurching from my right to left side, and then back again, sleep came. But along with it, a memory I'd suppressed for years sneaked into the room … and I was cold … so cold.

* * * * *

December 1941

Reports of the war raging across the oceans poured in as the year drew to a close. Despite the increasingly somber and concerned mood among my teachers and parents, we kids were somewhat oblivious. And while the Japanese dropped bombs on Pearl Harbor, more and more snow fell along the foothills of the Rocky Mountains.

New York City got snow, but nothing compared to where we lived in Colorado, especially on the west side of Denver.

My buddy Rick and I piled into the back of another senior's pickup to catch a ride to the top of Lookout Mountain to join the other thrill-seekers intent on racing down the mountain on inner tubes, sleds, toboggans, and even torn pieces of cardboard—anything that would whisk us downhill as fast as possible.

From the summit, the giant sledding hill spread out beneath me like a creamy white blanket. To the east, the big sky and wide-open plains stretched eternally. Behind, layers on layers of mountains stacked higher and higher until they seemed to cradle the sun and moon.

A natural clearing between the pines and an incline we swore went straight down at a ninety-degree angle, awaited all us kids lucky enough to escape chores and homework on a Saturday morning—sunny blue sky and a temperature so low your nostrils stuck together when you breathed. And while the kids perched at the top of the hill like eagles ready to soar, most of their parents waited below in the parking lot with thermoses of hot coffee, muffled in scarfs, and chit-chatting about whatever adults do.

As I stood at the top of the hill, overlooking the tops of snow-laden trees and the speckled buildings in the town below, a feeling of invincibility filled my mind. Perhaps it was the clear mountain air, free from the smog of New York City, but I was optimistic about my future for the first time in a while. Even though my parents whispered in hushed tones about my impending draft registration in a week when I would turn eighteen, my destiny felt safe on the mountaintop. I was still seventeen and had a lifetime to live.

Most of the little kids, bundled and nearly faceless, waddled to the left portion of the hill where the slope eased into what would be a grassy knoll in the summer. Along with the other teenagers, I vied for a position on the right, the steepest part of the mountain, carved along the row of trees that stood like spectators, waiting to cheer us on.

Tugging with alternating hands, I tested the steering mechanisms on my Flyer and ran numb fingers over the metal runners—knocking off the chunks of ice gathered from the long trek up the hill. With my eyes on the faint remnants of a track pressed and formed into last week's snow, the sled assumed its position, facing straight downhill and guaranteeing a thrilling ride.

I wrapped my scarf high over my mouth and nose and raised my coat collar to my ears. Just before lying on my stomach, another boy about my age pushed ahead of me. He wore a pointy, orange stocking cap and too-big boots with laces loose and dragging in the snow. Looking like a drunken carrot, he stumbled backward, stepping on the handles of my sled.

"Hey, watch what you're doing!" I gave him a shove. "You cut in."

His eyes watered and his nose dripped in tandem. "You ain't king of the mountain." He tugged the frayed rope attached to a rickety sled. "Whoever gets here first goes down first."

"You won't make it far on that piece of junk." To mark my territory, I pulled my scarf to the side and spit into the snow. "The nails will come loose, and the whole thing will fall apart before you make it down." I inched my sled forward, elbowing the kid to the side.

"I'll race ya. Make you eat your words when you meet me at the bottom."

We gave each other a stink eye as we lay side-by-side, heads downhill like compasses pointing due north.

The underlying snowpack and ice on the faint track would be the speediest route. A slight turn of my handle to the left would shoot me onto its path to dominate the race. Whoever this kid was, he was smart, or at least a seasoned sledder. Out of the corner of my eye, I caught him orienting himself in the same direction.

"On three?" He licked his upper lip with one swipe of his tongue. "One ... two ..."

Before he released the last word, I gave him a Herculean shove, jolting him and his sled to a sharp right angle. Laughing, I dug my boots into the snow and lunged forward, straight down the mountain.

As I neared the bottom, a cacophony of loud voices cheered me on—impressed with my speed and agility—my fearlessness to race down the mountain at break-neck speed. But as I slowed to a stop where the hill relaxed and eventually flattened, the panicked expressions on the faces of moms and dads, and those kids already down the hill, signaled they were shouting at someone other than me. A man in a black cap frantically waved his arms as if he were a giant bird caught in a windstorm.

As I turned to locate the crowd's focus, everything went into slow motion despite events happening simultaneously. An orange stocking hat flew parallel to the ground, stretched out behind a supine and aerodynamic boy, his sled teetering side to side like a tiny boat tossed in the white-capped waves. He was far off the intended hill, dangerously close to the tree line and rocky outcrops. Powdery snow covered his face as he picked up more speed before summiting a ridge leading to the entryway into the parking lot. A red truck, painted the same apple red as my Flyer, approached.

The driver never saw the boy shoot over the ledge and slide under the front wheels. But we all did. Men ran to the truck. Mothers held their children and covered their faces with their coat sleeves as a bloody and crumpled figure was pulled from under the vehicle.

A woman wearing a pale pink coat screamed—an agonizing sound, so guttural it echoed off the canyon walls. She ran, slipping on the snow and ice, toward the boy. A girl, about my age, ran after the woman, and together they slumped onto their knees next to the still body.

Slow motion slowed. Silence drifted over the valley. Everything was still.

Suddenly, the woman let out a piercing scream, reeled backward, and collapsed in the snow. Onlookers rushed to her side and gathered her up. But the girl draped herself over the lifeless body until, finally, the man with the black cap pulled her away. Another woman went to the girl. She secured the buttons on the girl's navy coat and pulled her hood over tangled brown hair—as if bundling her up would make everything all right.

Other parents attempted to console a man wearing overalls. He paced back and forth, his face ghostly white as three wide-eyed faces peered from his truck's back window.

Then, the girl in the navy coat turned toward me, her stare narrowing the distance between us until it seemed we were face-to-face. We looked at one another for what felt like several minutes while puffs of steam escaped her mouth and swirled around her face—expressionless except for the tears running down her windblown, pink cheeks.

The sled rope hung limp around my wrist. It didn't matter that my hands were numb. It would have been better had I not been able to feel at all. More than anything, I wanted to be the boy lying on the ground, my own blood spilling into the rutted road, seeping into the snow to hide the sin I'd committed.

Chapter Fourteen

Essie ~ I Knew You

Blame it on the wine and the tiramisu, but my indigestion was more likely a result of the uneasiness I felt about why Joseph was compelled to dash out the door. The evening had been so enjoyable— two mature, intelligent people having engaging conversation, sprinkled with humor, and seasoned with mutual attraction. *Salt and Pepper ... not a bad duo.*

"I hope he's all right," I spoke over the hum of the dishwasher. Tucking the wine glasses back in the china cabinet, my hand paused before latching the glass door. The crowd of salt and pepper shakers I'd collected over the years at thrift stores, garage sales, and on vacations stared at me. "Oh, Ray, you always hated these things—thought I was crazy to collect them." I rearranged two mini adobe-house shakers I'd bought on a trip to Santa Fe when the kids were little. "Never in my wildest dreams would I have thought about another man in my life, especially now. You think I'm crazy?" The silence provided no answer.

No need to catch the news. The ten o'clock show was nearly over, and the weather would do what it wanted, regardless of the shapely blonde meteorologist's magic screens. Instead, I settled on the sofa, tucked the fleece throw around my legs, and reopened the 1941 yearbook.

Faces met mine with pin-curled hairdos and combed-over, slicked-down, side-parted hair. Horn-rimmed glasses, buttoned-up shirts, and Peter Pan collars lined up across the rows of students. Some I remembered; most I didn't.

Esther Owens. My eyes settled on a youthful face. Brown, curly hair, pinned back on the sides with tortoise barrettes. A slight smile curved upward toward round, innocent eyes. The locket secured around my neck was from my mother for my sixteenth birthday in August, just before the school year began.

Pages turned past the sophomores and juniors to the senior section. For the boys, jawlines were more defined, and goofy grins from earlier years were replaced with serious looks—perhaps the realization that their draft number would soon come up, and the battlefields would replace their playgrounds and baseball fields.

The girls, too, appeared changed in only two years' time—full cheeks and lips framed by coiffed hair. Red lipstick emanated from the page, even though the photos were printed in only black and white.

Louis Rizzo. My finger stopped at his picture. "I wonder whatever happened to him." He was a handsome fellow—tall and muscular, with soft brown eyes and chestnut hair the girls whispered about when he passed them in the main hallway. Plenty of students came after the school year began, and several simply disappeared when their families had to move for more work. But Louis arrived—then disappeared—like a beautiful dream that slips from your memory.

Louis Rizzo, though rumored to barely mutter a word, and presumed to have come straight from Italy and therefore didn't speak English, though I learned later he and his family had moved from New York City, had caught my sixteen-year-old eye. Once, in the crowded hallway, we bumped into each other. I mumbled a faint *sorry,* and he replied something similar in Italian. After that, I watched for him in that busy hallway during passing periods, hoping to accidentally step in his way. Regardless, even though I only watched him from a distance— and it was a one-sided, imaginary affair—he was a lovely sight to me.

Before closing the book, Joseph's last words before he abruptly ended our date reeled back from the past ... *mi dispiace ... mi dispiace.* I stared at the face again. As if we locked eyes across a far-reaching horizon—across a sea of memories bobbing on the waves of the passage of time—I recognized him.

No. Couldn't be. Too much wine? His strange behavior.

And yet ... the eyes? *Joseph.*

Chapter Fifteen

Lou ~ Interrogation

Usually, I looked forward to my Sunday morning call with Jennifer, but today I wished I'd been delinquent on my phone bill and the service was cut off. Regardless, she'd find a way to track me down. The phone rang at 11:00 Mountain Time sharp, her East Coast 13:00. *She would have made a good officer. Precise.*

"Hi, Dad. How're you feeling today? Is this still a good time to chat?"

"Sure. It's the same time we always talk." I tore open a bag of saltine crackers and crushed one into my rewarmed, chicken-noodle soup. "And why do you always ask me how I'm feeling?"

"You sure are grumpy."

"Just because I'm old doesn't mean I'm sick."

"Let's start over." Her buttery voice she used as a young girl still melted me.

"I'm sorry, hon. Lots on my mind right now."

"Could it be the woman you've met? Online?"

"How in the world do you know anything about that? Did I say something last time we talked?" The passing of the days calculated in my mind. I'd only met Esther within the last week, so Jennifer wouldn't have known any more than me.

"Woman's intuition." Jennifer's voice flattened. "Actually, it was Arlene."

"She called to snitch on me?"

"No, I called her to see how things were going with the house. Thought you might need extra help with grocery shopping, laundry, maybe the yard. She figured you would have told me about this new venture. I was a little embarrassed she had to fill me in."

The coalition between Arlene and my daughter had me outnumbered, but stealth was my middle name. "I'll have you know I was the one who had to show Arlene the proper way to iron a shirt. I've been ironing my own shirts and pants—"

"Since the day I enlisted." A sigh followed. "I know, Dad. But it's perfectly okay to ask for a little help."

"If I need anything, I'll put out a Mayday. Until then, assume it's all hooah."

"But you should have told me about this dating idea, especially since you're gallivanting around the Internet. That's not safe, you know?"

"I'm a big boy. No one's going to kidnap me." My intended humor hung in the air like a kite caught in a tree.

"Since when are you on the Internet, or for that matter, the computer?"

"How do you think I ordered the genealogy profile I gave you last Christmas?"

"But dating? I don't know what I think about that, Dad. How would Mom feel?"

"She's not here to tell me." Without warning, the words erupted from a gaping hole I'd thought healed. "Besides, she can't feel anything since she's dead."

The words surged like a river of burning lava—unleashed, uncontrollable, and destructive.

"Daddy," her voice cracked.

From the first time I held Jennifer, she transformed my life. When Betty announced she was pregnant, not to mention both of us were nearing our forties and Michael was already twelve, I was shocked and admittedly not too happy. But when the nurse handed me the bundled-up featherweight, life bloomed again. All that mattered was the pink little face staring up at me like a spring blossom poking out of the garden. Ever since her arrival on a late spring day in 1962, Jennifer had been my bouquet—the sweet fragrance in my life.

Now my harsh words, like a clumsy gardener's oversized boots, trampled the flowers, snapped stems, and crushed the delicate petals. "I'm sorry, Jen." My throat tightened as tears that I'd thought dried up, pooled in my eyes, seeping from the tender places of my heart. "We both miss her."

Strange, how silence lingers between two people—suspended like a one-way bridge—until one person takes the right of way and approaches the other.

Jennifer took the lead. "How was your dinner date last night? Does she have a nice home? Is she a good cook? How late did you stay?"

"Good. Yes. Yes. Twenty-one hundred hours."

"Come on, give your little girl more than that. This isn't an interrogation."

"I beg to differ." My soup had cooled and would need reheating for the second time today. "And if you want to know the truth, this was all a dare by Hank—nothing serious, just a good ole buddy challenge for the fun of it." Hopefully, that would be enough information to throw her off track, and I could change the subject. "More importantly, what's going on with you and Carl?"

"You're not off the hook that easily, and you know Arlene will tell me everything." She sighed. "Anyway, Carl and I met for dinner last night. We caught up about the kids and synced our calendars."

"Sounds more like a high-powered business meeting."

"Maybe so, but Kristi is super stressed about making grades for her sorority, and Matt is thinking about a gap year after he finishes his engineering core classes this semester."

"He's taking a gap year after he's already started his degree? Doesn't make sense to me. Whatever happened to perseverance, gutting it out?"

"Lots of students take more than four years."

"And take more of their parents' money."

"Dad, maybe we should talk tomorrow. You seem a little edgy."

"Sorry. I just worry about you."

"Likewise."

A deafening blast sounded into my ear. "Jennifer, what's that noise?"

"My hairdryer. The girls from my yoga class are going out for a glass of wine."

"On a Sunday afternoon?"

"No, tonight, after I shoot another wedding this afternoon. Business has been booming."

"So, you do yoga on a Sunday night and then go out drinking?"

"Oh, Daddy. It's New York City. The night will be young."

"At least something is."

The wind-tunnel roar ceased. "I love you, Daddy. We'll talk next week."

Before I could get my words out, the turbojet revved its engine, followed by a static buzz. "I love you too, darling."

Chapter Sixteen

Essie ~ Checkpoint

By morning, I knew it wasn't the wine, and I was almost certain Joseph Marino was really Louis Rizzo. The list of reasons as to why he would lie to me about his real name didn't amount to much. Perhaps the deceit had to do with his lengthy military career—forced to change his identity for a top-secret purpose. Maybe it was as simple as wanting to ease into meeting strangers while dating online—remain somewhat anonymous until he was interested in someone for more than one meeting. After all, I went along with Allie's suggestion to use my formal name, albeit that wasn't too creative, to protect my identity.

My dates with Joseph totaled three, if I were to count the coffee-lunch date as two separate events. Why didn't he divulge the truth? To think, the one boy in high school able to make me swoon from afar was the same man whose life now intersected with mine sixty-one years later.

I picked up the phone, determined to find out not only why he lied about his name but, more importantly, why he'd left so suddenly—as if a ghost had entered the room. If this was a game, I too could be strategic and knew that two could play at cat and mouse.

* * * * *

"Hello." His voice was clear, not one that belonged to someone laid up in bed with a stomachache.

"Good morning, Joseph. Oh, I guess it's nearly noon." My demeanor was so sweet I may as well have been sucking on sugar cane. "Thought I'd call to ask how you're feeling. Such a shame you had to run out like you did. We were having such an enjoyable time."

"My apologies again. Hopefully, in all my agony I was able to thank you for a delicious meal and lovely evening." He paused. "That doctor of mine may be right—something's going on with the digestive system these days."

"Are you well today? You sure sound better."

"Umm. Yes, thankfully so. Not perfect, but better."

"Then the vegetable soup I made for you will be the right medicine." I tapped my fingers on the countertop. "I'd like to bring some over before it gets cold."

"I won't be here." His words were rushed. "Catching the last church service."

"Oh? I wasn't aware you attended." Clearly, he didn't want to see me for some reason. "I'll leave a Tupperware on the front porch. You can reheat it later. We live pretty close, but remind me of your address."

As though revealing top-secret information, he slowly recited the address as I jotted the information on a piece of paper.

Now, I needed to whip together some vegetable soup.

* * * * *

The American flag flying near the front porch confirmed I was at the correct house. This time of year, when the weather cooled and the days shortened, most folk laid aside their patriotic duty, stowing flags into closets and garages until the Fourth of July rolled around. A retired Army colonel was not one to stow away the flag.

In the event he was home, I checked my hair in the rearview mirror and took a deep breath before exiting the car. The home was pretty, red brick with green shutters and a matching front door. The remnants of summer's perennials lay dormant, waiting until next spring to color the garden again. Leaves were raked into neat piles, evenly spaced along the walkway, just as I imagined his subordinates stood at attention awaiting his orders. I lifted the brass doorknocker and let it fall from my fingers once, then twice.

As I expected, no answer. With the container of soup settled on the teak bench near the door, I peeked in the glass panes. The foyer appeared dark, no one shuffling down the hall to greet me with a broad smile—the one he wore on his face most of last night. What happened between us settling side by side on the sofa holding hands and his supposed gut issue? Is dating me a game to him?

The yearbook. Maybe Louis Rizzo had more to hide than his name.

Chapter Seventeen

Lou ~ Covert Mission

Like a compromised reconnaissance mission, I watched from the upstairs bedroom window as Esther pulled in front of my home. Esther. Essie. Which name didn't matter now. I knew who she was and hoped to God she didn't figure out who I was.

Not that she could hear me, but I held my breath. Undetected. Stealthy. Clandestine. Was I acting childish? I snickered at the possibility despite my age. Maybe she'd decide to drive away before I passed out. No such luck. After what must have been a hair combing and freshened lipstick moment, she emerged from the car.

It would be impossible for her to miss Old Glory when she came up the walkway. Who wouldn't be struck by the red, white, and blue waving in the wind? Plus, she was patriotic—another thing I liked about her. And the leaves … the job should have been completed a few days ago, but my back doesn't agree with bending over to pick up the piles like it once did. Maybe Arlene would help me with that next time she came. I hope Essie doesn't think I'm lazy.

As quickly as Essie ascended the path toward the front door, she descended the path back to her car. I felt my face redden. I was ashamed—hiding in the house like a coward, unwilling to at least tell her face-to-face that our short-lived dating relationship was over.

But you don't want it to be. The realization caught me off guard. I knew it was true. In the short time since we'd met, an undeniable and renewed energy bubbled in me like an underground spring, rocks pushed aside, and free to quench what had been parched for too long. Kindness, beauty, and … excitement. Those elements were pure Essie—

the seasoning my life needed.

No time to contemplate, I raised the window and called her name, and this time the name mattered.

She stopped and turned, first looking back at the door. Then following my whistle, she glanced up.

"Hello, Esther. I nearly missed you."

"I thought you were at church."

A hint of sarcasm dangled on her comment. *She had smarts too.*

"I'm on my way down. Give an old man a minute or ten." I'm not sure why I laughed, but seeing her again, even from a bird's-eye view, lit a spark in me that had been extinguished when Betty died.

With each downward step, I wondered how I would end my charade if we were to continue seeing one another. *Maybe Joseph Marino is my new persona. He's not that bad, after all. He doesn't have to know about Esther Owens and what happened to her brother.*

A hand may as well have slapped me across the face. I stopped on the last step and sighed. *Got myself into a mess with this lie, but I am no liar. I just need time to make my plan.*

Before I opened the door and would be face-to-face with Essie, I resolved to talk tomorrow with Hank. Perhaps after all these years, it was time for me to come clean about my past, at least with one other person, someone who knew the despair of ending another's life. In that sad, yet unique way, Hank knew me better than anyone else. Plus, he'd be honest with me—tell me if I really was as unredeemable and unforgivable as I'd believed for so many years.

"Sorry to keep you waiting." I straightened my sweatshirt. "I was dressing when you rang the doorbell."

"I knocked." She air-knocked a couple times. "Maybe you didn't hear while … um, putting on your workout clothes."

As she eyed me head to toe, I suspected her next comment and was prepared to be a step ahead. "The church I attend has one of those—"

"Informal services?" She grinned. "Maybe I could join you sometime. I like to keep an open mind. You know, not be too dependent on a certain pastor or praise and worship team."

My face must have appeared as blank as my mind. Suddenly, my throat felt as though I'd swallowed a wad of cotton.

"Joseph." She wrapped her fingers around my forearm. "Are you okay? You're looking a little pale."

I cleared my throat. Little did she know she had provided the alibi that would keep me in the clear … at least for a while longer. "Not at top speed yet. Probably best I stay home and take it easy today. Tomorrow I'll be a hundred percent." I lifted the Tupperware from the bench. "And I'm sure your soup will be the remedy." *God only knows I don't need more soup.*

"Nothing fancy, but I hope it helps you feel better." Her eyes had a lovely way of squinting when she smiled. I'd noticed that about her right away at the coffee shop. The sun had shone in the window next to where we sat and illuminated her eyes—mostly blue with hints of green. She had defined cheekbones and soft, pretty skin—fewer wrinkles than her age dictated. Right away, I found her to be beautiful.

"Ess … Esther," I stammered as though my mouth had two left feet. "I'd ask you to come in but—"

"It's all right. I came here to …" She paused. Then she tilted her head to the side and closed her eyes as though carefully contemplating her next words. "Drop off the soup."

She shrugged. "Maybe call me sometime and let me know how you're feeling." She lifted her hand and gave a half-hearted wave as she walked away.

I blinked a few times. For someone whose words came easily, I was speechless. *Sometime* meant no time if I didn't respond. *But then the past could stay the past. She'd never know who I really was. I'd never see her again.*

Never see her again? I felt a lump in my throat that had nothing to do with my loss for words. Instead, the thought of never seeing her again made me sad, empty … so lonely that my heart actually ached. *Say something, you big fool.*

"Date?" I sounded like a monosyllabic caveman. By her quizzical expression, she must have thought the same.

"Excuse me?" She stopped.

"Would you go on a date?" *A little more dignified.*

Esther turned and looked at me. She was quiet for several moments, a good reason to brace myself for the rejection. Justified on her part. I'd acted like a crazy man last night, and now I didn't even invite her into my home for a cup of tea or coffee.

"Yes." She nodded as though her common sense had conceded. "And I suppose that date would be with you, *Joseph.*"

The emphasis on my name was not mistaken as I watched her get into her car and drive away. Esther White. Essie Owens. The girl with the pink, windblown cheeks and navy coat had become not only a beautiful elderly woman but an intriguing one at that. And of all the women in the world, she was the one, after sixty plus years of me hiding, to find a second key into my heart.

Chapter Eighteen

Lou ~ Comrade

Since Viva Dolce is closed on Mondays, Hank and I decided to be ambitious and go for a walk in the park. More like a saunter with his bum hip, but still covering ground.

"Let's grab this bench and let the other pedestrians lap us." Hank plopped on the bench, his long legs stretching onto the gravel pathway.

"That'll be easy for them considering we haven't made the loop even once." My left knee let out a pop as I settled next to my friend. "Getting old stinks."

"We're not getting old. We are old." He slapped my thigh. "But we have our minds. That's a good thing."

"Agreed." We sat in silence for a few minutes, taking in bike riders zooming by, an extremely happy golden retriever walking its owner, and three young mothers running behind aerodynamic joggers.

"Don't mothers simply push strollers on walks anymore?" My gaze followed the blur of swinging ponytails and neon tennis shoes down the path. "Babies must grow up with their faces all pushed back—like they've been raised in a wind tunnel."

Hank pulled back the sides of his cheeks. "Like this?" He let out a laugh—the same one that kept things light when the stress and fatigue of our army training got the best of us.

"Times have changed, buddy."

"Agreed," I echoed.

"Speaking of our minds, what's on yours?"

Yesterday, while I ate my umpteenth bowl of soup alone and kicked myself for not inviting Esther to join me, I rehearsed my disclosure to

Hank over and over in my mind. Imagining her across the kitchen table, the same spot where my wife and I shared our morning coffee, seemed natural—like it was finally okay for someone else to be in her place. A first step ... if only I wouldn't keep falling into the pit of the past.

"Do you believe in fate, Hank?"

"I suppose so. But how do you mean?"

I cleared my throat. "Like one move to the right or left, up or down ... that slight motion could determine the direction of one's life."

Hank rotated toward me. "Sure. That happens." His eyes drew together, deepening the wrinkle between his brows. "Happened to me on Mount Belvedere. In an instant, I stepped to the left, Private Timmons followed ..."

My friend remained in his thoughts until I joined him. "Behind you?"

He nodded. "And took a bullet to the chest." His hand rose to his own as if feeling the pain. "Died a few minutes later."

"After all these years, doesn't get easier, does it?"

"To tell you the truth, I hadn't thought about that kid for years. Used to think about him often. Real funny guy. Joined the Division shortly after you left for officer training. He'd get us laughing so hard at mealtimes that food came out of soldiers' noses. Made us laugh even more. Then the farting and burping started ... a real ruckus ..." Hank smiled, reminiscing about brotherly bonds born in hard times. "That private would have made some woman mighty happy had he had a chance to marry. Only wish I hadn't stepped to the left, leaving him room to follow."

"But you didn't make it happen ... it just happened." My mind reeled, trying to make sense of the sequence of tiny moments in life that have monumental outcomes. "Fate found its site. You couldn't change it."

"You're right, the Kraut had his sight set on that exact spot. I happened to step out of it, and Private Timmons stepped in." A deep sigh followed. "That's what I've had to remind myself over the years. When other good men fell around me, or the enemy was on the receiving end of my bullets and grenades, it was fate's doing, not mine."

The bench was cold on my back, giving me reason to freeze up and say nothing more to my confidant.

"Hank ... I killed a boy." There, it was out, released like the first leak of air from a balloon before being pinched closed again.

"I'm afraid we both did. That was our duty."

"No." More air released. "Before the war ... on a sledding hill. We were in high school." Deflated, I told Hank the rest of the story—every detail etched into my memory like a fine lithograph. Even the girl in the navy coat, staring at me at the base of a snow-packed sledding hill. The same lovely woman with hair as pure and white as salt that I couldn't get out of my mind.

When the last words were shared, I may as well have run around the park a hundred times as I felt my ball and chain had finally been cut free.

Hank was quiet for a long time. His eyes were closed, and I wondered if he was catnapping. But when he muttered an "amen" and crossed his legs, I realized he'd been praying, and I could only assume he'd been talking to God about me.

Hank squinted an eye. "Remember when we first met, 1942, Tenth Mountain Training at Camp Hale?"

"Sure, I do."

"I asked if you could kill someone, and you said you didn't know if you could."

"Yah, I remember saying that ... and I meant it."

"I know you did." He cracked his knuckles, the same distinct sound I'd heard each night from his bunk above mine.

I shifted on the bench, not sure where my buddy was going with this.

"Lou, you aren't a killer ... not then, not now. Let the past take its rightful place ... in the past."

"*Sempre Avanti*," I whispered the Division's creed. "Always forward, right?"

"You got it, my friend. Keep moving on, keep focusing on what's ahead, not what happened in the past ... *always forward*."

"Something else I need to say." I cleared my throat.

"Let me guess." He playfully raised clenched fists. "You're in the Italian mob, and I better watch my back now that I have dirt on you."

I rolled my eyes.

"Seriously. What is it, Lou?"

"I don't understand why I'm still here and others are gone. I should have died several times over but was spared."

"You're a cat? Nine lives, or something like that." He tilted his head. "Just kidding. I'm listening."

"The avalanche." I shuddered at the memory of Hank and me skiing on the ridge above the barracks. Without any warning, the giant slab of snow broke loose, and, like a rushing river, carried me down the mountainside until I was buried, unable to move as if in cement.

"I'll never forget. Nothing like I'd ever heard or seen before."

"I couldn't breathe. Didn't know which way was up or down, and the weight on my chest was like nothing I'd ever felt. Before I knew, I heard scraping and opened my eyes to see you staring down at me."

"Prettiest mug you'd ever seen."

"If I could have used my broken arm, I would have pulled you down and kissed you smack on the lips." I puckered my mouth.

"In hindsight, maybe I should have left you buried." He punched my shoulder.

We sat quietly for a few minutes, and, if like me, we replayed the terrifying scene in our minds, thankful we could joke about it now.

"And the Philippines, the shoreline between San Jose and the Daguitan River." I held up my hand. "Bodies all over the beach, and all I left there was my thumb and part of a finger. When the blood oozed out of the hole in my hand and dripped into the sand, I thought how poetic my ending would be. Just as I was responsible for life draining out of the boy at the bottom of the snowy hill, mine would seep into the sand." I rubbed the remnants of my hand before continuing.

"Crazy, but I remember thinking how difficult it would be to hold, never mind aim my gun. I hoped my end would come quickly, at the mercy of a sharpshooter or a haphazard bullet." I folded my hands together, gathering the words to describe the most painful part of the event. "But as if someone, perhaps God Almighty Himself, made me aware of a fellow soldier moaning only yards away, I knew it wasn't my time to die. I gave myself a swift kick in the pants, ran to the man, and heaved him onto my shoulder."

Amazing how a distant memory can stir emotions. I pulled a handkerchief from my back pocket, wiped my eyes, and cleared my throat to finish my story.

"Most of what happened next was a blur. Somewhere among all that chaos … the shouts, gunfire, heavy machinery, and plumes of disrupted sand, I collapsed into a grove of gnarly bushes. The thorns. I remember they ripped through my uniform like razor blades. The soldier, and he looked so young … he looked up at me … I'll never forget his eyes. It was if he was pleading with me to say something. I told him help was on its way, and he'd be all right."

"No luck?"

"No." I shook my head. "After a few minutes, he relaxed, too heavily, into my arms."

Hank slowly nodded, and I wondered which of his own battles he was visiting.

Again, we remained silent as if the past needed time to digest, allow our stomachs to settle like after a mess-hall meal gone bad.

"There's more. Years later when my family and I were stationed in Germany during Vietnam …" Hank patted me on the thigh, a little heave-ho to give me permission to keep going.

"I left my office fifteen minutes earlier than usual to catch my daughter's school performance—a bomb detonated and my staff were killed. I've probably told you about that day, but not the reason I wasn't sitting at my desk at the moment it was blown to bits. Should have been me, Hank, not the others."

My friend shook his head and then covered his face with large, knuckled hands.

I didn't expect him to have the answer, or for that matter, know what to say. I'd never shared those thoughts and the associated guilt that dangled over my head like a noose—taunting me with the memory of the sledding day, or whenever a soldier, friend or foe, lay lifeless in a puddle of mud or the swaying grasses of a field.

"Probably time to go." I flattened my hands on the bench. "Thanks for listening to me ramble."

"Then listen to me." He grabbed my forearm with a strength he must have reserved from his army days. "Tell Essie the truth. Let her know who you really are." His words were more an order than a suggestion. "If not for her, then for you. From the first time we met, something's been chewing away at you." He uncrossed, then crossed his legs again. "Time to come clean. Time to forgive."

"I can't expect her to forgive me. She'll hate me … and I can't blame her."

"That will be her decision." Hank narrowed his eyes and stared me down like a company commander. "But you have to decide if you're willing to forgive yourself … 'cause quite surely, God forgave you long ago."

"You believe that?" I rubbed my palms together, and, despite the cool breeze, they were clammy.

"I do." Hank leaned back and stretched his arms to the sky. "But now you have to be honest with Essie. That's the right thing to do."

Like withered perennials after a long winter's rest, we stood and walked toward the car.

"I'm curious, though," Hank pondered. "The day it happened, did she know you were the one who caused the accident?"

I stopped, considered his words carefully. "Don't know. Not that it matters ... because I know."

Chapter Nineteen

Essie ~ Second Chances

When the voice message from *Joseph* suggested our date be the Denver Art Museum, I assumed he was trying to earn back some much-needed points. Regardless, if he was attracted to me, the feeling was mutual, and to up the ante, my curiosity about his pseudonym kept rising.

Over our first dinner date, I'd talked about a recent museum exhibit by Zen priests, including hanging scrolls, folding screens, and lacquerware. Although the rare items were fascinating, my real desire was to reconnect with the rich history of Western art—sculptures by Remington and Proctor—and spend time with a favorite, somewhat inconspicuous oil painting by Worthington Wittredge. The eighteenth-century artist's name was reason enough to study his work.

As soon as we arrived at the museum, we headed to the north building and the Petrie Institute of Western American Art. No need to tour the entire facility—Modern, Asian, African, European, and the host of other worthy exhibits could wait for other days. Besides, I preferred to ingest art in smaller morsels and savor the taste.

"Beautiful, isn't it? *Foothills Colorado*." I spread out my arms as if embracing the piece. We sat side by side on the low bench, facing the painting on the lapis-colored wall. "Unlike most of his contemporaries, who preferred to paint grandiose mountain ranges, Wittredge was enamored by the prairie."

Joseph cocked his head to the side. "The artist was on to something. The way he painted the foothills, rising up behind the plains. In their own right, they're as spectacular as the high, snowcapped mountains.

Those lower hills would be easy to overlook, but this guy captured them well." He leaned closer to the painting. "Funny … it feels like I've been at that exact spot some time in my life."

"Maybe a time long ago, before everything changed around here." I ran my finger along the artist's quote in the exhibit brochure. "One would be impressed with the vastness and silence and the appearance everywhere of an innocent, primitive existence." My eyes took in the array of color and texture in the small painting, but my mind drifted elsewhere—back to the town of Golden, a stone's throw west of Denver and nestled in the foothills of the Rocky Mountains. And high school— the long-ago era and innocent time. Why, if Joseph Marino was really Louis Rizzo, would he keep his true identity a secret, especially now that our lives had intersected all these years later? It was all so confusing, but this man intrigued me, and an attraction existed between us— regardless of his name.

Drawn away from the landscape on the wall, we looked at one another.

"It *was* an innocent existence, right, Joseph?"

He was silent for a few moments, his eyes squinting despite the soft lighting in the gallery. Then, as if a raw nerve was struck, he flinched and rubbed his forehead.

"There's a lot I don't remember … besides, we were only kids." He pushed himself to a stand and took my hand. "Let's walk. Shall we?"

We strolled past some other paintings—stunning oils of Native Americans and weathered cowboys—and paused at Henderson's *The Chaperone*. It was a large canvas with an interesting composition of three people—a young man and woman, and an elderly woman between them.

"Too bad that poor man couldn't take an evening walk with his gal without the nosey woman wedged in between." Joseph tucked his arm around my elbow and pulled me closer. "Would have told her to take a hike so I could kiss the girl."

"Aren't you the romantic?" My smile came naturally. It felt good to be perusing the museum with another instead of my frequent solo visits. I had invited Phyllis and Ginny to join me, but they preferred making their own art, paired with wine, laughter, and paint-splattered smocks.

Even before Ray passed, my annual art museum membership was stamped "individual" as my husband was more interested in military collections and displays filled with old guns, swords, and wartime machinery. But Joseph seemed genuinely interested in the display, and we strolled in sync as we paused to read gallery notes and attributions.

We entered the adjoining Western Sculpture room. Remington's *The Cheyenne* leaped across the room on horseback as Proctor's famous *Buckaroo* sent a cowboy reeling. A roomful of history in motion, yet each piece perfectly still.

"Amazing how real they look." Joseph circled the bronzes, running his hand along the glass cases. I wondered if he desired to reach out and become part of the scene.

I understood that power—art so real and captivating that I'd yearned to become part of it—step into a field of towering sunflowers or meander a rainy city street.

He cocked his head to the side and squinted at me. Had he read my mind?

He continued, "Everything, even down to the expressions on the faces … the hair, the—"

"Hands?" My arms, palms open, extended toward Joseph. "Take my hands, Joseph."

His face was drawn, as though presented with a perplexing and complicated puzzle. "Not too comfortable offering my lame hand, dear." He extended his right hand, the usual one I'd held since our dinner date.

"Let me hold both of your hands." I reached toward his left until, hesitantly, his fingers touched mine.

"Not a pretty sight." His voice wavered, almost apologetically.

Ever since I'd noticed his injury on our initial date at the coffee shop, I realized he usually kept it tucked away in a pant pocket or beneath the table at mealtime. Was his hand a prelude to other hidden things?

"That doesn't bother me." With his hands in mine, I gently ran my thumb over his thumb on the right hand. On the left, I felt the gnarled bump and thick-white scar that replaced where his thumb and forefinger had been before the war. My eyes followed the raised veins, enlarged knuckles, and wrinkles—badges of old age similar to mine.

"Esther, why are you doing this?" His voice was barely a whisper, and except for the uniformed security guard who'd passed by minutes ago, we were alone.

"Because I had to make sure." I swallowed hard. "Had to make sure you are—"

"Louis?" As if the blood in his veins turned to ice, he froze and stared at me.

"Yes. Louis Rizzo." I wasn't sure the words even surfaced as my legs shook and my hands grabbed his forearms.

He didn't respond at first, his eyes moistening, until he took my face in his hands and kissed me. Not a peck, but a passionate kiss—mutually desired.

If being swept off one's feet is truly possible, I was close. Sea legs found me far from any shoreline. "I must say, that was quite impressive." My face had surely reddened. "But why did you do that?"

After his brave move, I would have expected the man to be grinning from ear to ear. Instead, everything about his demeanor was serious, perhaps even somber.

"Because if I didn't kiss you, I'd regret it forever." Shaky fingers ran through his silver hair. "I understand if you never want to see me again."

A giggle sneaked out before being caught. "Do you think I'm that much of a prude ... not willing to kiss a man who's stirred my heart from the first time I saw him?" I gave him a short kiss on the lips. "But you owe me an explanation for lying about your name."

"Esther, do you *really* know who I am?"

"I believe so." Now my demeanor was serious. "You're the handsome, senior high school boy who never noticed the ogling, awkward sophomore girl."

"I must have been blind."

My fingers went to his cheek, and for a moment, my mind drifted to 1945 in the stateside hospital where I was an operating room nurse. "And you're the soldier who came back from war with a bandaged hand, but most likely his heart hurt worse."

He glanced around as though clearly confused at my revelation and looking for answers.

"I wouldn't have expected you to notice, much less remember me from high school. When I finally got the nerve to go into your room to introduce myself, you were sound asleep. Then my shift was over, and the next day, you'd been released." I sighed. "Figured I'd never see you again."

I turned my back, forcing my eyes to study a painting of a dilapidated barn. The knotty wooden boards, droopy eaves, and peeling paint reminded me I'd weathered as well, but like the barn, I too was still standing. I breathed deeply, relieved that memories from my past, like the winds that coursed through the high canyon walls had finally reached the wide, open space below and dissipated to a calm and meandering breeze.

As I continued looking at the painting, I felt his hand rest on my lower back. "Figured it was fate that I was the nurse on duty the day you arrived for surgery." The memory replayed in vivid color against the backdrop of my white uniform, the bleached patient gowns, and the cold, stark operating room. "The only difference between who I knew you to be then and who you are now is you went on to become a dedicated husband, a loving father, and eventually a wise and wonderful older gentleman." I turned toward him and our eyes locked. "And here we are now ... *Lou.*"

Now it was his turn to breathe deeply. He pressed his lips together. "Yes, my dear. Here we are and—"

A docent with a brood of schoolchildren, followed by a harried teacher, entered the exhibit room, signaling our peaceful museum outing was over. After I situated my purse strap on my shoulder and Lou donned his jacket, we made our way to the exit arm in arm.

Chapter Twenty

Lou ~ Grace

Hank was a talker, but he didn't always have a way with words. I wanted him to confirm that I was off the hook from the past and free to run headlong into the future with Essie.

"She figured out the real me." I pressed the speaker button on the phone and continued to make a pot of coffee. "Found my photo in the high school yearbook and could see right into my lady-killer eyes."

"That's what she said?" His voice was gravelly over the speaker. Perhaps I'd awakened him earlier than usual from his slumber.

"Not exactly about the eyes, although she did recognize me … something about our eyes looking at each other across time and space." I glanced at my three remaining fingers. "And she remembered me from the hospital after returning from the Philippines. I don't remember seeing her, but I was coming out of surgery and probably didn't have my wits about me anyway."

"Over sixty years ago? Her memory must be sharp."

"That's the truth. She was a nurse at Denver General for thirty years. Did I mention that?"

"Not that I recall."

"Hank, she knows I'm Lou Rizzo, but … she doesn't know I killed her brother." My coffee cup clattered on the counter, spilling a small puddle on the laminate.

"You sure?"

"Yes."

"How so?"

I folded, unfolded, then refolded the dishrag as I pondered his question. Could Essie be that angelic that she'd forgiven my trespasses? Could she have gone through deep psychological therapy and reconciled with past trauma?

I grabbed the dishrag and threw it in the sink. "If she knew what I did … who I really am, she'd hate me and would have every right to slap me across the face and tell me where to go."

I took Hank's nasally breathing as agreement. "Did you hear me?" My right temple throbbed, pressing on my mind like a vice grip. "I planned to tell her everything. Like you said, get it off my chest so I could be free from the memory and come clean with her."

"Did you?"

"No. After the museum, we went across the street to Civic Park. We agreed we needed fresh air even though it was chilly and the homeless folk kept stopping us for money."

"Many of them vets?"

"I suppose so. Vietnam for sure." I shook my head, recounting the numerous indigent men and women roaming the park looking for handouts and a place to huddle as the temperatures dropped. "Essie and I talked about the yearbook, the hospital … how life has a strange way of reconnecting people. Then, she asked about the fake name."

"And?"

"Told her about the dare with you and how the whole dating idea was crazy at first—that it seemed a good idea to go incognito. Didn't think I'd meet someone again who I cared about."

"Do you care about her, Lou?"

The question was simple, but it forced me to pause and reflect. "I do, Hank … deeply." A subterranean level, untouched since my years with Betty, had shifted. "I may even love her. Sounds crazy being that we've only dated a short time, but there's something really wonderful about her."

"Then tell her the whole truth, buddy."

"I figured you'd say that, but you realize I'm risking her ever wanting to see me again, and—"

"And your chance to be loved again?" His voice was flat.

"Is that all bad? We know time isn't on our side." My left temple throbbed in syncopation with the other. "This may be my last chance to—"

"Live again?"

Live. Again. As though a knife cut through his words, separating them into the two hemispheres of my mind, I weighed each carefully. *Live.* By most standards, I'd lived a good life. Did more, seen more, owned more than most people around the world. Beautiful wife and kids, good job, good health, and good friends. I dodged death more than once and had the wrinkles to prove it.

Again. Was I so bold to want even more? Was I deserving of a second round of happiness? An additional helping of fond memories, laughter, and tender touches? Somehow, despite what I had done to another person's life and the lives of those who loved Edward Owens, my life was playing out like a triple-header baseball game. But as selfish as it seemed, I hoped for *again.*

"Lou?" Now, on the other end of the phone, like a faithful dog on a leash, my old war buddy and best friend waited for my answer. "You still there?"

"This is a second chance, Hank, and I don't want to blow it."

"Understood, Lou. Just consider this. Perhaps what you've been offered is more than a second chance. Maybe it's something greater than that."

"And what would that be?"

"Grace, my friend. Grace."

Through muffled words, we said we'd talk soon. It was my turn to be silent as I leaned my elbows on the counter and buried my head in my hands.

Chapter Twenty-One

Essie ~ Trust

"Excited for your date tonight?" Allie called from the adjacent dressing room. "Still can't get over your crush on him in high school and reconnecting in the hospital. So weird. I'm definitely writing that into one of my books."

Our biannual-birthday-shopping tradition had been happening for so many years that styles had been in and out of fashion. The mall outings began when Allie was old enough to care about clothes, and I was wise enough to accept that Ray could not choose flattering clothing for me. Like so much of what Ray and I did, we had learned to walk in stride with one another—not always in step.

"Yes." My reply came out as a grunt as I wedged into a skirt, clearly mismarked as a size larger than it was. "Lou's been nothing but a gentleman, and in hindsight, it makes perfect sense that he'd want to hide his identity until he knew me better." The zipper retaliated, forcing me to admit defeat. "You should have counseled me to do the same."

"I did!" A high-pitched retort sounded through the thin divider.

I shimmied the skirt to the floor and kicked it to the discard pile. Before leaving the dressing room, I'd perform my usual ritual—re-hang, re-button, and re-zip. Tidy up, be responsible … bring order … control my surroundings.

"Mom, if you recall, you fired me as your ghostwriter." A knock followed. "Eureka! I've found something that fits. Open up and take a look."

I cracked the door and peeked out. "Oh, honey." I smiled, probably the same silly grin as when my daughter wore her empire waist, raspberry-colored prom dress, and eventually her wedding gown—princess-style, of course. Now as a middle-aged woman, she was lovely in black fitted pants and a muted, floral print blouse. The best part was her complimentary smile, nearly ear to ear.

"What do you think, Mom?" She turned in a circle. "Peter might like this."

Why a lump formed in my throat, I wasn't sure. Seeing my daughter happy and spending time with her all these years—doing simple things together, just like breathing—filled me with life. "You are beautiful, dear. Stunning. Peter should be proud to call you his wife."

"Thanks, Mom. Funny thing … he told me that last night."

No more words were needed as we both smiled—understanding the deep need to be loved.

* * * * *

Fortunately, our shopping mantra—Shop 'Til You Drop—didn't include the latter half, and I made it home in time to freshen up and slip into a new blouse and pant set. Never mind that I'd succumbed to the elastic-waist variety, cutting off garment tags and donning a fresh outfit satisfied the soul.

"As always, you look stunning." Lou presented me with a lovely bouquet of red roses. "A beautiful woman should never be without flowers."

"Sir, you spoil me." For the past two months, my home had been adorned with fresh flowers. Most definitely, the florist at City Market and Lou were close friends.

"Brings me joy." He uncorked our favorite wine and filled our glasses. "I have an idea. How about we take a cooking class? The gourmet store in Old Town has Italian lessons on Tuesday and Thursday evenings."

"Don't you like my cooking?" I feigned a pout but wondered if last week's lasagna wasn't up to par for his Italian heritage.

"Love your cooking." He patted his belly. "I just thought it would be something fun for the two of us to try together." His hands rested on my hips as he began a slow, swaying dance. "Adding the ingredients, mixing it up, turning up the heat in the kitchen—"

Playing coy, I gently pushed him away. "You doing the dishes …"

"That too." He let out a peaceful sigh and grinned. "Essie, I'd go to the ends of the earth with you and back again. That's how happy you've made me ever since we met."

"Lou Rizzo, I feel the same about you." I raised my glass. "Salute."

In return, he raised his glass. "*Cin cin, amore mio.*"

"And I have an idea as well." I ran my finger around the rim of my glass, considering the best way to proceed. "Would you consider going with me to church on Christmas Eve? I realize your daughter and her family will be in town, and I'm not sure what Peter and Allie plan to do since he always works late that day. Can you imagine still doing your shopping on Christmas Eve? Maybe you prefer to go to the Catholic Mass and—"

"Essie, stop." He shook his head definitively. "It's all right. I'll go to church with you. I'm not a heathen, you know."

"Of course not. I wasn't implying—"

"Besides, Hank already hit me up." He sipped his wine. "He and Libby are going and asked if we'd like to join them."

"That's nice of them. They seem to be serious these days."

With a finger to his lips, he whispered, "He's asking her to marry him on Christmas Day. Putting a ring under the tree in a fancy wrapped box." Lou dropped his jaw in a pretend shock.

"That's so romantic." I touched the bare spot on my finger where I'd worn my wedding band for fifty-six years.

Lou must have noticed as he took my hand in his and held it to his lips. "It brings me great joy to know you were happily married as I was. No marriage is perfect, and we'd be fooling ourselves to say there weren't hard times." He kissed my fingertips. "But I was always faithful to Betty, and I'm sure you were to Ray." He nodded as though pressing the commitment and its value deep into his soul. "Trust. One of the main ingredients that kept us together all those years. Kind of a rare commodity these days, but worth its weight in gold."

Chapter Twenty-Two

Lou – Conviction Calling

The sanctuary brimmed with the beauty of the Christmas season. A giant, white-lit tree garnished the majority of the altar, and wreaths with red satin bows adorned each window. Children bounced up and down on the pews, most likely more excited for Santa and gifts than Jesus in the manger. An entourage of musicians and singers made their way onto the stage while I shifted in my seat and wondered why I had agreed to all of this.

"Seems more like a concert than church." I nudged Hank, who was sandwiched next to me with Libby to his left. "Lot different than the Catholic Mass." Essie, seated to my right, smiled and nodded.

"All the same God." Hank winked. "He's glad you're here."

"Me and all the others who only come on Christmas."

"You might like it. Never would have thought I'd find myself wishing Sunday morning would come sooner. Like waiting for the best meal of the week—it fills me up."

"You don't say?"

"Getting filled by the Spirit. Best nourishment I've ever had."

The music began—a piano, bass, lead guitars, keyboard, and even drums. Two women and a man began singing, and the audience stood and joined in. On Essie's cue, I pulled myself to a stand and found myself clapping along.

"You didn't say this was going to be an exercise class," I whispered in her ear.

"Keeps us old folks awake." She squeezed my arm. "They'll slow down with Christmas classics after a few more songs.

After "Joy to the World" and "Hark! the Herald Angels Sing," a man in slacks, a button-down shirt, and a red tie stood behind the podium.

"That's our head pastor," Essie said.

"Good to know. I was expecting a guy in a long, white robe."

A few minutes into the sermon, the man could've been standing in front of the crowd wearing only polka-dotted underwear. His words captivated me; in a strange sort of way, he seemed to speak directly to me.

* * * * *

After we exited the sanctuary, Hank and I waited in the foyer for the ladies to serve Christmas cookies they'd helped bake earlier in the week.

I nudged Hank. "Interesting what the pastor said about grace." Talking about faith was never in my repertoire of conversational topics, and I was surprised when the sentence slipped out.

"What did you find interesting?" Hank bent over slightly, positioning his good ear toward me as the crowd around us had grown.

"He likened it to a gift. Given free of charge because God loves us." I rubbed my chin, trying to recall the exact details. "Awfully generous of God … especially since I'm a sinner."

"You and me both." Hank chuckled.

"Remember me talking about a second chance?" I lowered my voice despite the growing crowd. "And you brought up grace?"

"God's grace." He nodded. "You've beaten up yourself long enough for something you've considered a sin … maybe it was, maybe not … perhaps only a tragic accident." He gave me a firm pat on the chest. "Lou, God knew your heart then, and He knows it now."

I glanced up at Hank, who, despite both of us losing a few inches over the years, still hovered over me. "I'll need to think about that some more, but I'm beginning to understand."

If eyes can smile, Hank's did. For the first time, the notion registered that our friendship was due to a power beyond simple coincidence. Like a favorite sweater—darned together long ago as young men, threads unraveled and pulled apart as life took separate courses, and then woven back together as we aged and needed a comrade for comfort. After all these years, we wore our friendship well.

"But don't take too long only *thinking* about God's grace." He rested his arm on my shoulder. "If you decide you really believe, act on it.

In a chorus of laughter, Libby and Essie joined us, bearing thickly frosted cookies speckled with red and green colored sugar. A short while later, we said our goodbyes and Christmas wishes to the other couples, then Essie and I made our way through the parking lot—two old people, holding hands, and madly in love.

As I drove Essie home, Hank's last thought lingered on my mind like the gentle snowflakes gathering on the sides of the road, blanketing my world with a fresh and pure slate.

Chapter Twenty-Three

Lou ~ Unwelcome Call

The phone rang on my nightstand, and I grabbed for it in the dark. "Hello," I mumbled.

"Lou, it's me, Essie." Her voice was strained, not the usual melodic tone.

Must have been from the years in the barracks, but I was out of bed in seconds and flipped on the light.

"What's wrong, doll?"

"It's Hank. Libby just called. Something about his heart, or a blood clot. Oh, I don't know for sure. She said she tried to call you but somehow got the numbers mixed up. Good thing she and I exchanged numbers awhile back."

* * * * *

The past has a way of playing cruel tricks in the middle of the night. Tonight, as I clutched the receiver, another dreaded call replayed in my mind.

The night the news came, Betty, Jennifer, and I were living off base in a quaint town with aromatic flower boxes on windowsills and lively beer gardens on street corners. Even though the war in Vietnam raged and the casualties continued to mount, we were apart from it on some level, yet bound by a taut rope—a noose of sorts—until our son was safely home from his tour of duty.

"Honey, turn it off." Betty yawned and snuggled closer to me. "We can't watch the news every night."

The broadcast was in German, a learned language for me. However, regardless of the dialect, the images were universal. Death and destruction spoke to all.

Jennifer slept in the small room down the hall, probably dreaming the songs she and her classmates would perform the following evening at the American Academy Springtime Performance. I'd promised to leave the base in time to watch her dance, and as my wife and I kissed goodnight and closed our eyes, I hoped I'd be able to stay true to my word.

At zero two hundred hours, the phone rang. It wasn't unusual to get calls late at night, especially if something was up at the base, but this time, I hesitated to lift the receiver.

"Aren't you getting it, Lou?" Betty's voice was groggy.

I swung my legs off the side of the bed and answered the phone. "Five, six, eight, three, eight."

With my identity rattled off, a familiar voice spoke, "Lou, it's me, Colonel Watson."

"George. It's been awhile." The last time I'd heard him speak was at my commencement as I advanced to Colonel when he was my senior advisor and mentor. "You still over in 'Nam?" He sounded far away amongst the static, and I realized this wasn't a casual call.

"Too long, buddy. And yes, I'm still in this hell-hole." Silence hung between the thousands of miles separating us. "Even though I requested permission to reach you, I hate to be the one to call."

As though standing on a cliff, realizing loose rock and earth were giving way, my heart stopped.

"Your son ... Michael's been killed." Static followed, swallowing his next words. "Darlac Province ... clear and search operation ... I insisted ... reach you as soon as possible."

Whatever he said next was a blur, as though a horrific monster stormed the house, consuming me and everyone that mattered in one foul, painful gulp.

"Who's on the phone, hon?" Betty tugged at my elbow. "Is something wrong?"

I grabbed her hand and squeezed it tightly. "Thank you for making the call, George. I'm sure it was difficult."

"My duty and honor." He cleared his throat and then more static. "Hopefully, when ... other side of this ... peace ... Lou ... tell Betty how sorry I am."

"Will do." Quietly, I settled the receiver into its cradle, wishing with every ounce of my strength the call was a cruel nightmare.

When my wife's eyes met mine, she knew the purpose of the call. A mother's instinct is supernatural. Without me saying a word, she knew our son had died. As I pulled her tightly to my chest, her tears soaked into my nightshirt as mine dampened her hair.

The next morning, two uniformed Army officers arrived at our home. Following protocol. No need for small talk. We knew why they had come. First a salute, followed by a nod to Betty. The tall, pale one delivered the news.

"Colonel Rizzo, Mrs. Rizzo … I have been asked to inform you that your son, Michael Rizzo, has been reported dead in Zone C, outside Katum, South Vietnam at 01900 on August 26, 1969. He and three other soldiers in his platoon were ambushed while patrolling the perimeters of the encampment. On behalf of the Secretary of Defense, I extend to you and your family my deepest sympathy in your great loss."

Even though Betty and I trudged through the day mired in thick fog, we agreed not to tell Jennifer right away about her brother. Seven years old is young, and while the world was spinning out of control, she deserved the innocence of childhood—to sing about new beginnings and springtime as she danced in her homemade butterfly wings—believing they would magically lift her above the stage if she fluttered fast enough.

At the office, the tragic news spread quickly among my fellow officers, and they ushered me off the base earlier than usual. Considering I was spent to the core and needed to check on Betty before she took Jennifer to the school for the performance, I obliged and left the base at sixteen hundred hours.

At seventeen hundred hours, the house phone rang. Again, my identity code was shared before Major Barkley spoke. "Sir, there's been an explosion at the base."

"Specifics, Major."

"Your office, sir."

"Anyone hurt?" Against all my years of training, my voice trembled. "Casualties?"

"Yes sir, two and one unaccounted for."

"On my way." I slammed the phone down and raced to the carport. "I'm sorry, Jennifer," I spoke to myself as I turned the ignition and threw the car into reverse. "There's no more innocence left in this world."

★ ★ ★ ★ ★

My weary family of three returned to the States—not to a joyous homecoming but to pay condolences to three women, each granted the unwelcome label of widow at the hands of German terrorists.

Standing in Arlington National Cemetery at the newly dug gravesites of my fallen comrades, the never-ending rows of white markers, aligned in perfect, soldier-like attention, were surreal. Had those men not insisted I leave the base early that day, I would have been sitting at the exact spot where the car bomb drove through the wall and exploded—obliterating my desk, body, and everything else within a thirty-foot radius.

With head bowed, I hoped a prayer would come on behalf of these good officers, and even better men. But I couldn't shake the suffocating weight. A shroud of guilt convinced me that fate made a fatal mistake, and I should have been the one lowered into the ground. Instead, death missed its mark again. It should have been me, not my son, who stepped onto a hidden land mine and had life stolen away.

The next day, Betty, Jennifer, and I flew home to Colorado, Michael's home as well. His final resting place at Fort Logan National Cemetery was marked by another slab of white marble, etched with the lifespan of too few years.

* * * * *

Nearly forty years later, my knuckles turned white as I gripped the receiver. "Is Hank—"

"They've put him in ICU. We can't see him, but Libby's a mess. She's hoping we can be with her and pray."

Pray? Did people really pray for one another? When the other, long-ago event awoke Betty and me, there wasn't any reason to pray. Already too late. Our son was dead, his lifeless body wrapped in a bag, eventually to be transferred back to the States.

"I'll pick you up." My pajama bottoms were already tossed on the floor and my nightshirt unbuttoned.

"No, that will take too long. I'll meet you at Saint Anthony's Hospital. You know where that is, don't you?"

"Got it, and Essie … be careful driving. The roads will be slick."

"You as well. And, Lou, I love you." The phone went silent.

* * * * *

Hospitals, especially late at night, aren't my favorite place. But when it's my best friend who's in trouble, my own issues don't matter. After making my way through the zigzag corridors, I saw Essie and Libby in the waiting room, holding hands with heads bowed.

I felt awkward interrupting their sacred time—a private conversation with God—but when Essie looked up and forced a smile, I knew this was the right place to be. Hank, who lay in a room somewhere behind closed double doors, needed support that only those who love one another can provide. The three of us hugged. That unique human gesture capable of warming the heart.

Essie took the lead. "The doctor spoke with us a few minutes ago. Said Hank has a pulmonary embolism. Not a massive one, but serious enough they have him on blood thinners and all sorts of drugs."

Libby's face was drawn, her eyes bloodshot and skin pale. "Hank and I decided to continue to celebrate Christmas Eve together." She pursed her lips. "Thank God he came into my house, or this would have happened as he was driving home alone."

Essie continued for her friend, who was blotting her nose with a well-used tissue. "He couldn't breathe very well and said he had a sharp pain in his chest. Scared her to death when he started coughing and couldn't stop." Essie patted Libby's forearm. "That's when she called nine-one-one."

"The paramedics let me ride to the hospital with him. Said they never had someone in such pain talk so much on the way to the hospital."

I couldn't help but smile, even though my nerves were frayed with worry. "That's our Hank."

"But then he got quiet once we arrived. I knew something serious was happening." Libby stared at the closed doors. "Wish I could be with him. Doesn't feel right to have any space between us."

"Let's pray for him again. That will help bridge the gap." Essie took Libby's hand and then mine. I followed suit and grasped Libby's hand. As they took turns speaking to God in soft voices, I shifted my weight from one leg to the other, trying to get comfortable in our intimate circle. Whether or not the ladies waited for me to pray, especially during moments of shared silence, I only listened.

I hadn't spoken to God directly in years and assumed he didn't want to hear from me now. The last time, I called out in fits of anger and regret—cursing him for allowing my son to die while I sat behind a desk, pretending to carry on another day, another duty, far away on another continent.

Chapter Twenty-Four

Lou ~ Face-to-Face

Days became a mishmash after we visited Hank in the hospital. Christmas Day had come and gone, and a new year would begin in a few days. Once he was moved out of ICU, the three of us took turns at his bedside so Libby could rest. Libby and Essie preferred to read to him and take command of the television channels to search for, as they said, "a show with decent merit and no filth."

My preference was to sit quietly with my buddy. No words necessary. Of course, even when Hank wasn't at his peak, I should have known silence with him would be temporary.

"Did I scare you?" He opened one eye like a scruffy pirate with scraggly facial hair.

"No, you're a tough old bird. This is tiddlywinks compared to what you've come up against."

"It scared me." He turned his head on the pillow. His eyes were glassy, not the crystal blue I was used to seeing. Typically, a witty comment would follow, but he remained serious. "But then it struck me on the way to the hospital that I'd be going home, and that wouldn't be bad at all."

"Home?"

"Heaven."

"Oh, that home. The biggie." My smile must have turned from lopsided into a smirk, because Hank, despite not sitting up in several days, grabbed his bed remote and nearly launched himself into an upright position.

"Hey, go easy with that thing. The nurses will take away your toy."

My attempt to make light of his change in demeanor wasn't working.

His eyes, usually kind and inviting, shot darts at me. "No more pussyfooting around with you." He pointed a long, arthritic finger at me. "I'm the one who nearly keeled over in front of the woman I love and plan to marry. Now I'm lying in a hospital bed, got doctors poking and prodding me, and you're the one I'm worried about."

As my only defense, I crossed my arms and legs in unison. "And what's that supposed to mean?"

He was quiet for a few minutes, and I worried if he'd overdone it with his bed-bound gymnastics. Finally, he spoke, with the same compassionate and authentic tone I'd first heard at Camp Hale when he assured me we'd be friends for life. "It's time you forgive yourself." He leaned his head into the pillow. "All these years, you've been so wrapped up in guilt and busy condemning yourself, and do you know what you've missed?"

My raised eyebrow begged the answer.

"Grace."

"That concept's been popping up lately."

"Maybe the Big Guy's trying to get your attention before it's too late."

"You make it sound like I might die any second." Looking around the room at all the medical equipment gave me pause. "Suppose we never know for sure, do we?"

"Nope. Who would have thought a blood clot would have let loose and lodged in my lungs? Before that moment at Libby's, I was feeling fine."

"So, are you going to ask her to marry you?" My strategy to move the subject away from my eternal outcome was risky—Hank was keen.

"Already did."

"But you had the ring wrapped under the tree for Christmas morning."

"Still do, and when I'm out of this place, Libby and I are going to open gifts just like we hadn't skipped a beat." As casually as riding down the escalator at the mall, he lowered his bed. "The thought of proposing to her got me so excited that I couldn't wait any longer … asked her before we met you for church on Christmas Eve."

"And you kept it a secret. Impressive."

"Nearly had Libby jumping out of her skin, though. We decided unwrapping the ring together the next morning would be the best Christmas present ever." His heavy eyelids fluttered shut a couple of times. "Just didn't plan on ending up in the emergency room."

"Time for you to rest, buddy." I patted his hand, careful not to bump the intravenous line dripping a concoction of drugs into his fragile system.

"Lou." He gripped my hand. "If it feels right, pray for me."

My eyes burned, and a lump formed in my throat. With my half hand, I overlapped his and held it tightly. "I'll do that, brother."

After I left his room and his door closed behind me, I walked down the long hospital corridor. *If it feels right,* Hank had said. For the first time in my life, I wanted to pray, not spew a rehearsed prayer from a childhood memory, not curse God's name for taking loved ones from me, but actually talk with God, meet Him in a place where my fears and preconceptions were set aside and my heart could rest in His hands.

Chapter Twenty-Five

Essie ~ What to Say?

Getting off the hook to meet Lou's daughter and family was short-lived. The plan was to spend Christmas Day together. However, with Hank's hospital escapade, Jennifer, Carl, and the kids decided to extend their vacation in Vail and join us down the mountain at the end of the week.

When Lou met Allie shortly after we'd begun dating, he'd gotten off easily. She was enamored with him from the first meeting. Bringing a bouquet of sunflowers to Allie was a smart move, although unnecessary. Lou was eloquent and charming—a perfect gentleman—and could have stepped out of one of Allie's novels as the hero.

Peter and Lou bonded as well. A shared love for Europe and history kept their discussions lively for hours, and living close to them allowed the relationships to grow naturally.

Now the time had come for me to pass inspection on Lou's turf, and the Meet-the-Family was minutes away. At any moment, his family would pull into Lou's drive in their SUV rental, and it would be game on. The twins, and most likely Carl, would be an easy victory. Jennifer, an only daughter and daddy's girl? She might be a tough opponent.

"You okay?" Lou corralled me by the hips as I fussed around the kitchen, wiping the countertops and overfilling a bowl of chips. "You seem jittery."

"Too much caffeine. I should stick with the decaf herbal blend."

"You're not nervous about meeting my family, are you? They may be a little nutty but harmless." He made a silly face. "Now Jennifer, she has a bit of a bite."

"That's what I'm afraid of."

"She'll be fine." He waved his hand, brushing off my concern. "She just worries about everyone and everything. The twins, Carl, me, the weather, the financial forecast, if she's missed her exercise class … you name it, she worries about it."

"Understood. Then she and I might get along just fine."

"When she found out about Betty's cancer and watched her mom decline so quickly …" Lou's shoulders stooped. "Jennifer tried to be strong and hold everything together, for her mom, for me. But I wondered if she was falling apart inside." He gazed out the kitchen window, perhaps visiting the past. "And though she was a little girl when Michael was killed, that was hard too."

I joined his gaze, allowing a momentary toe-dip into the icy waters of my past. "I'm sure it was. I often wonder how Allie was … and is still, affected by losing her big brother, especially since she was never able to have her own family. People handle those things differently now."

"What do you mean?"

"Counseling, group therapy, all the self-help books that tell you how to solve problems and overcome obstacles."

"You're right. Things are different now." He scratched his head. "I suppose back then, even though sometimes it feels like yesterday, our only help was to just keep living."

"And here we are." I squeezed his hand. "All right, then. We have hungry guests arriving."

* * * * *

After plenty of hugging and handshaking, the conversations turned to who fell the least on the slopes, skied the fastest, and ordered the best tasting beer at Pepi's Bar and Restaurant. A competitive spirit hovered over Lou's family—unlike my tiny clan, more concerned with yielding the right-of-way.

"Since when can you two order beers?" Lou pointed at Matt and Kristi.

"Papa, we're in college." Matt's smile was broad—charming like his dad's.

"But you aren't legal." Lou spread his arms, waiting for further explanation.

"And neither were you, Daddy," Jennifer interjected. "Don't let on like you didn't drink underage in the Army. We've all heard plenty of stories about you and your soldier buddies."

"True. You got me on that one." Lou raised his hands in surrender. "Hey, did I tell you about the time—"

"Ugh!" a unanimous moan followed from Lou's crew.

So, I wasn't the only one who heard lots of stories about the seasoned soldier's Army days. Fascinating for sure, but long. "How about we eat?" I motioned to the table. "I'd love to hear more about each of you."

The twins were doing well in college—Kristi studying journalism and advertising, hoping to follow in her dad's footsteps at a flashy agency in New York. Matt was the outdoorsman; his ideal life was to work in forestry, live in a remote cabin in Rocky Mountain National Park with no indoor plumbing, have five dogs, and in his words, a hot wife. Lou understood the intrigue of the Colorado mountains but wasn't as confident about his grandson's desire to find a hot wife who shared the same dream.

Carl was on the reserved side, but his words were thoughtful and kind—clearly an intelligent, contemplative man whose hard work and creativity had earned him a leading position at the ad agency. No one mentioned his health challenges, but his hand trembled when he lifted his fork, and he seemed tired, yawning several times and stretching back in his chair. Perhaps the altitude and week of skiing were too much.

After brunch, Lou herded Carl and the grandkids to his office to show them his war medals and medallions—a repeated event when relatives and friends visited from out of town. Jennifer started on the dishes as I wrapped up the leftovers.

"Your dad tells me you enjoy yoga." A topic related to relaxation was a sure bet.

"It's my therapy. I try to catch a class at least four to five times a week." Jennifer rolled her shoulders back several times.

"Good for you. I wish I could say the same. I try to make it to Pilates or catch a Silver Sneakers class a couple of times a week."

She raised an eyebrow. "Silver Sneakers?"

I straightened my back, silently admitting I hadn't been to a class since before Christmas. "It's for us well-seasoned people." I smiled, hoping she'd return the gesture.

"Dad says you're close to his age." As she paused and looked me over, I had a funny sensation I'd walked through an airport scanner.

"That's right. I'm eighty."

"Well, you don't look a day over seventy. Keep on exercising. I'm a firm believer it works."

"Helps with stress, right?"

She shot me a questioning look. "Did Dad tell you about Carl and me?"

Lou had mentioned several times his concern for his daughter and son-in-law's future. It wasn't for lack of love—they'd met in college, married as soon as graduation hats were tossed in the air, and the twins came a few years later. The skyscrapers of New York City became their fairy-tale castle—an exciting life, blessed with Carl's high-paying, high-profile advertising career, Jennifer's blossoming photography business she'd begun when kids started elementary school, and the twins doing well in school and excelling in a myriad of activities … all was great until Carl became ill.

As her husband's health declined, Jennifer's worry and anxiety grew—especially regarding Carl, and her dad, far across the country.

Unclear how much I should be privy to, I attempted to skirt the question. "I'm not sure … by the way, Matt and Kristi are lovely, young adults. You must be so proud of them."

"I am." Then she corrected herself. "Both of us are." She paused, letting the water run over her hands. "Neither of them gave us much trouble. Just the typical things kids will do. Carl worked such long hours … still does, really." She turned the water off and dried her hands. "Wish he wouldn't do that. I'll admit, I get lonely with the kids out of the house."

Wanting to be careful where to tread, the only words of wisdom that came to me were "marriage and family are complex, hills and valleys."

"How long were you married?" Her question was weighted.

"We'd just had our fifty-sixth anniversary when my husband passed away."

"That's a long time. Mom and Dad were together fifty-eight years." She faced me. "But you probably know that."

"Yes. Your dad tells me your mother was a wonderful person. He loved her very much."

Jennifer was pretty—classic features reminiscent of the Estee Lauder makeup model. Slightly older, but aged like a Renoir portrait, flawless.

"She was a wonderful mother and a good wife." Her eyes moistened, and she dabbed at them with the dish towel. "I miss her every day."

Motherly instinct urged me to hug her, but until we knew one another better, might be better to remain on the other side of the chasm, apart from the sacred place of a mother and daughter's love.

From across the void, I offered words of confirmation. "I'm sure you do, and I know your father misses her too."

"Essie, can I ask you something?"

"Sure." I tried to sound casual, but my own stress-bearing muscles between my shoulder blades tightened. "What would you like to know?"

"If he misses her so much, then why has he fallen in love with you?"

Intrinsically, I knew Lou loved me—we'd shared the sentiment with each other nearly every day the last month or so. But to hear it spill from the mouth of his daughter caught me off guard. My heart wanted to assure Jennifer that her father was in good hands with me— not a money-seeking, crazy old woman hoping for a free ride on the last stretch of road before heaven. But the pointed question deserved a truthful answer, not only for her but, most importantly, for Lou and me.

Refusing to be rushed and say something defensive, I arranged my thoughts, beliefs, hopes, and dreams like a beautiful bouquet. "Your father and I understand that love isn't reserved for only the young." I stepped closer to her. "Dear, love knows no age. It simply knows what's in the hearts of those who choose to embrace it."

Jennifer appeared lost in either her own thoughts or my brief dissertation. I stood next to her, drying the last of the pots and pans.

"Thank you for being honest." Briefly, she touched my forearm. "And for being a good companion for my dad."

"And thank you for allowing me to be honest." I waited for more words to spill from her partially opened mouth.

"You know I love my dad."

I nodded.

"After Mom died"—she wiped the counter in swirling motions, over and over as if the rhythm helped her collect her thoughts—"it's been my job to take care of him. You know, keep close tabs on his health, make sure he's staying social … look out for his best interests."

"And you've done a great job." I spread my arms wide. "Even with the distance between you."

Jennifer's mouth pinched as she folded her arms across her chest. "Essie, Daddy and I are very close, and nothing will ever change that."

"Jennifer, I only meant the distance across the country, not your relationship with your dad." I walked halfway around the center island, giving both of us needed space. Clearly, I'd touched a sore spot and wasn't sure exactly what or why. Was it me? Another woman besides her mother stepping in for the proverbial last dance?

In my mind, I wrestled with the right words to say but came up short. Maybe no response was better. Jennifer had turned her back to me, busying herself with prepping a pot of coffee. Instead of pushing the conversation, I dimmed the overhead lights, agreeing our talk was over.

"Essie," Jennifer's voice was quiet.

I paused, questioning whether I heard her at all.

She turned and looked at me, eyes filled with tears. "I'm sorry."

"It's all right, I under—"

"No, I shouldn't have said that. I just worry about Daddy, and I don't want him to be hurt. It was so hard to lose Mom and the thought of him falling in love again and then—"

"Losing again?" I propped my elbows on the counter and rested my head in my palms. "Believe me, the same thought has crossed my mind. Why in the world would I want to risk losing another person who I love deeply, especially at my age?"

Her eyes widened as if she hadn't considered I could feel the same way.

"I'm not a gambling woman, Jennifer ..." I sighed. "But I'll take a chance with your father. He's a good man and worth the risk."

Like me, she propped her elbows on the counter and rested her head in her hands. With only inches between our faces, we breathed in unison—a silent treaty between two women who dearly loved the same man.

"Essie."

"Yes."

"I don't think I'm strong enough to lose the two most important men in my life." She seemed to stare past me, into the future, into the unknown.

"You will be, my dear." I took her hands in mine. "But we aren't there yet."

Chapter Twenty-Six

E ven though the doctors reminded Hank he wasn't the perfect picture of health, he and Libby didn't want to postpone their wedding.

"Give me one reason we should," Hank said when I'd asked if he was sure about making a huge commitment. "Why wait around for the perfect time to love again?"

No reason for argument on my part, so I'd assured him Essie and I would arrive on time to be the best man and matron of honor. Since most of Hank's family members had long since passed, only an out-of-state cousin or two remained, I was the closest blood to him. Our shared past and solid friendship earned me family status. And my secret, though nagging and unresolved, branded us as brothers.

* * * * *

Hank and Libby's small ceremony was as beautiful as their love for one another. Making small talk with Essie as we exited the sanctuary, I wondered if there existed a bigger plan for our own future.

"They'll keep each other young, don't you think?" She held my hand in an easy sort of way.

"You know what they say; the eighties are the new seventies. Pretty soon, the nineties will become the new eighties." With a pivot as fast as an eighty-something can do, I spun Essie around and put my other hand on her hip. "It's called the Decade Shuffle … the latest rage."

Our own dance, albeit a slower version, ensued in the church foyer until the church secretary interceded and laughed. "And you two weren't even the bride and groom."

I gave the lady my best wink and escorted Essie out of the church.

As we drove, Essie rested her elbow on the edge of the open car window and leaned into the warm spring air, her hair brushing off her forehead like a young girl out for a ride.

"Let's take a drive into the high country," she said. "Silly living so close and not going all the way up there. Plenty of snow still." She pointed toward the white-capped peaks. "But the roads will be dry."

Her adventurous spirit was one of many reasons marriage had been on my mind. The turnoff for the highway heading west, the main thoroughfare that would guide us to the evergreen clad slopes, rocky outcroppings, and winding roads approached—the same route to memories of the sledding hill.

"I have a better idea." Merging to the right, I exited the highway and turned the car east, away from the mountains and toward what I hoped would be a new beginning. "This might be crazy, but we're going to make two quick stops at our homes, grab a small suitcase, swimsuits … you have a swimsuit, don't you?"

"Probably buried in a drawer someplace." She gave me a blank look. "That thing hasn't seen water since my aqua aerobics class at the Y when I was … well, sleek and slender."

"You still are." I patted her thigh. "Grab the suit, a toothbrush, an outfit or two for going to dinner, and thongs."

She giggled. "You mean flip-flops. Not the skimpy pair of underwear I saw in the mall when I was shopping with Allie. I don't see what purpose those tiny things could serve. That is one item that definitely won't be in my suitcase." A clicking sound followed, reminding me that by many standards, particularly in the undergarment department, we were old-fashioned. "By the way, where are we going that we need such items?"

"Mexico, baby." With my sunglasses lowered, I cocked my head, movie-star style. "Must be flights all the time to Cancun. Surely there's room for two love birds who need to fly south for a getaway."

"Lou, this is what I love about you." She leaned back and smiled. "And a whole lot more."

"Likewise, hon."

"But Lou …"

"Yes, doll."

"You're forgetting I live in Evergreen." She jabbed a thumb over her shoulder. "*Up* the hill."

At the next exit, I turned the car around and headed west to retrieve Essie's beach attire. The extra time spent in the car was welcome and provided more opportunity for me to ponder how to whisk us away on a romantic vacation ... and formulate what I intended to do once we arrived.

* * * * *

One never tires of a stunning sunset, and as the orange ball floated on the horizon, I wished it would linger.

"Beautiful, isn't it?" Essie's profile was sun-kissed from our second day at the beach. Unlike the other older women who shielded themselves under floppy-brimmed hats and white, doily cover-ups, she'd waded into the ocean, spun in circles with arms wide, and then plunged headfirst into the water. She emerged, white hair slicked back and mouth smiling wide, like a mythical dolphin from Atlantis.

Now that the day had waned and the beach was mostly vacated, I reached across the small gap between our oceanfront lounge chairs and took her hand.

"What would you think about us getting married?" There, I'd stepped to the other side of what my daughter told me was nuts to consider. Jennifer insisted she liked Essie, understood why I had feelings for her, but the thought of making the relationship permanent had abruptly ended our last phone call. She didn't understand the necessity of marriage at my age.

"Is that a discussion point?" Essie turned toward me. "Or should I consider that a proposal? Albeit a weak one."

A muscular man and a bikini-clad woman passed in front of us along the shoreline. I followed their zigzag stroll in the sand for a few moments while considering my answer.

"I'm serious about the subject, but let's talk about it first." I swung my legs around so my face was inches from hers. "Besides, an old-school romantic like me can do a much better proposal than that."

"Good to know."

A light breeze cooled our sunburned shoulders, and Essie wrapped herself in the beach towel. Wearing my unbuttoned Hawaiian-print shirt—tucked away since a fiftieth wedding anniversary vacation to Oahu with Betty—and faded swim trunks, a sudden feeling of freedom and abandonment swept over me. *Must be what the pirates felt like—not a care in the world.*

"Let's walk along the beach." I stood and held out my hand. "The moon will be bright just for us."

* * * * *

When walking in sand, time loses its normal pace, and distance is irrelevant. We didn't care whether miles or yards were measured. All that mattered by the time we turned around and headed back to the resort for showers and then a seafood dinner was our mutual decision to marry.

"What do you think Allie will say?"

"She's a romance writer." Essie kicked playfully at a tuft of sand. "You have it easy." She stopped, pulling the towel closer around her middle. "The million-dollar question is what will be Jennifer's reaction?"

"She's a tough nut to crack for sure—huge heart, but so sensitive. She always has been." I rubbed my hands along Essie's shoulders. "But she'll warm up to the idea."

"And how long will that take?" Her eyes cast downward, as if she regretted her words. "I'm sorry. She's in a hard place right now. She's scared about what might happen to both men she loves."

Her question was fair, but I didn't have an adequate answer. The bond between a dad and daughter is one of the true wonders of the world—strong, complex, and mysterious. Forged at birth out of a need to protect. Delicate like the wildflowers woven through the little girl's long, tangled hair. Sealed with insurmountable strength when you release her at the altar into another man's arms, and miraculous when she brings new life into the world.

The best response I could provide was a gentle kiss. "I'm starving. How about you?"

Barefoot and half-dressed, we trotted off to get ready for dinner.

* * * * *

Tomorrow, on our last day of vacation before returning to reality, I would come clean. The getaway had been perfect and confirmed our shared love. But I resolved, before slipping an engagement ring on Essie's finger and professing sacred vows, that she would know the truth.

Regardless of whether she would still love me and want to marry—which at our age would be until death do us part—my sin would be forgiven. After nearly a lifetime of guilt, I finally understood. It wasn't a second chance that I'd needed. Instead, it was so much more. It was grace—a previously elusive gift that through prayer and private talks with God had entered my life.

After walking Essie to her room, I stood on my balcony and breathed in the salty air. The moonlight cast a white glow on the satiny sand below, reminding me of newly fallen snow. This time, it was peaceful.

Chapter Twenty-Seven

Lou ~ Coming Clean

Morning came quickly. As the sun ascended, ready to bathe vacationers with its warmth, Essie and I slurped the last of our mango, pineapple, and banana smoothies and headed toward the ocean for our last day at the beach.

Today, my destination was further along the coast, away from the lotion-lathered bodies aligned in rows like bacon on a platter. I motioned for Essie to follow me to a small inlet surrounded by rocks where the waves crashed in, sending sprays of saltwater onto the sand.

We listened to the ocean whisper of hidden treasures, seafaring adventures, and mysteries of the creatures that know it as home. The waves, methodic and constant, announced themselves with bravado, then subsided, rolling onto the sand as if eager to touch our toes—a gentle coaxing, a reminder that time had come for me to tell my story.

* * * * *

She listened to what I said, staring into the ocean, eyes focused on some faraway place.

"Do you see the waves hitting the rocks?" She spoke matter-of-factly, and at first it struck me as odd that she wasn't angry or crying.

She continued speaking in the same tone. "Each time a wave comes in, it's slightly different from the one before. Some roll in softly, barely lapping the rocks. Then the next comes in with such speed and power it pushes the water high on the shore, grabs a piece of driftwood, and pulls it back into the sea. Fascinating."

She paused as more waves approached the land, obediently

marching toward their destination. "The direction of each wave has a different outcome—not bad or intentional." She lifted a seashell from the sand and ran her fingers over it—dry, bleached, and broken.

"Once, this had life in it."

"Essie, I'm so sorry." My heart ached for her and the truth that was now part of her reality. "You had to know. All of it should have been said long ago." I pushed my fingers deep into the sand where its coolness met my fingertips. "For all these years, I couldn't bring myself to go there again and hoped what happened would go with me to the grave."

She looked at me, her eyes moistened. "You were an angel … at least that's what I wanted to believe." She squinted, perhaps reliving the scene. "I knew who you were from school even though you didn't know me. Seeing you in the hallways, I thought you were the most handsome boy alive. And then, at the most devastating moment in my life … there you were. Louis Rizzo."

My head pounded and I rubbed my forehead. "I don't understand."

"When I saw you, standing in the snow next to your sled and staring at me, I wanted to believe God sent me an angel who understood my fear and pain."

The memory was indelible—the girl in the navy coat with the tangled brown hair. "But even though you couldn't have known, I was the one who caused the accident." My eyes welled with tears. "Never in the world did I know one move, one change in direction would have such a horrible outcome." My face contorted at my confession. "Because of me, your brother died."

She pushed herself to stand and brushed sand from her swimsuit cover-up. As if retracing steps into the painful past, she walked away from me, leaving footprints along the shoreline as the waves did their best to erase them.

I wanted to go after her but assumed she wanted to be alone—surely to wrestle with the decision whether she could allow me to be a part of her life. But, as the distance between us grew along the water's edge, my desire increased to comfort her and tell her how much I loved her. With equal determination, though lacking in grace, I headed down the beach after Essie.

She had stopped at a small tide pool and sat on weathered rock, her legs dangling and feet submerged in the shallow water.

I settled beside her. To my left, remnants of a crab lay scattered on the black rock, most likely picked apart by the sharp beak of a sanderling.

"Essie, I understand why you can't forgive me and the hope of us being together is"—I swallowed the word—"please believe that more than anything in the world, I wish I could go back."

"He died because a little shift in the universe happened." She lifted a broken shell. "Don't you see?"

Through moist eyes, I tried to focus on the small object in her hand.

Her voice was soft, barely audible above the rolling waves. "Lou, you're not to blame."

I swallowed hard, trying to comprehend her words.

"Like this shell that once held life." She paused, holding it to the sun, its translucent edges illuminated. "At some point, a wave carried it to the shore, propelling it away from its natural course and onto the sand where it couldn't survive."

My gaze shifted to the broken crab. I wondered if it somehow knew that's where its life would end.

She tucked the shell into my hand. "That's what I believe happened to my brother. That's what I *have* to believe. Because, if I don't ... if I ... don't ..."

She said no more. She didn't need to explain. If she considered only the facts of what I said, then could there be no forgiveness, no love extended from her to me?

Chapter Twenty-Eight

Essie ~ Footprints in the Sand

Being old-fashioned has its advantages. As I expected, Lou had been the perfect gentleman and insisted I have my own room when we checked into the hotel. I agreed and was especially glad early this morning before the sun had risen.

A ghostly gray blanketed the beach when I put on a sundress and sweater and walked down the curving path to the beach. When the stone walkway ended, I slipped off my sandals and stepped barefoot into the cool sand. The sensation was soothing and refreshing, not yet scorching and painful as when the sun was overhead. I sighed, enjoying the momentary escape after a fitful night's sleep.

Like an overstuffed filing cabinet, the mind has an amazing way of sorting difficult memories and stuffing them into deep, musty places, pushed into the farthest recesses until something, or someone, yanks the drawer open. Records of past wrongs, mistakes, and sins flutter out—caught on the wind and scattered for the world to see. After Lou and I had said goodnight, and I lay awake alone in bed, my past was unleashed.

The beach chairs were stacked, nestled overnight until sunbathers dragged them to the prime waterfront views. In the dimness, I lifted the top chair and pulled it through the sand toward the steady hum of the ocean. Powerful, yet peaceful. Ebb and flow. Constant since time began.

I adjusted the top of the lounge chair so I could sit upright and stare at the dark sea. It seemed to move in slow motion—a giant serpent ascending from a faraway, unknown place—prowling on the earth's surface before descending with the light of day.

"Still running away, aren't you Essie?" I was startled by my own voice. The memories. As much as I'd tried to evade them, they'd pursued me all these years—like looking in a rearview mirror and seeing the haunting moments of my life chasing me. Although I was enveloped in darkness, I squinted toward the water—only shades of black and gray, speckled with silver moonlit highlights, punctuated the acute, painful moments of my past.

* * * * *

February 28, 1968

The last tray of peanut butter cookies, branded with crisscross fork imprints and sprinkled with sugar, lay on the counter when Reece came into the kitchen. He wore an odd expression—a mixture of confusion, anger, and somewhere in between happiness and relief. A torn envelope and letter were crumpled in his hand.

"They don't want me." His eyes met mine before shifting to Allie wearing a smudge of flour on her cheek. "I didn't pass the physical."

My instinct was to throw my arms around him and shout how happy I was at the news. Of course, my premeditated strategy was to act surprised if the results went the intended way, even though my plan was nearly foiled by that incredulous nurse.

"Reece … I'm not sure what to say." I reached for the letter. "Here, let me have a look at that."

The letter was pointed and formal, a notation near the end referencing the reason for being denied service in the United States Army. *Congenital platelet function defect.*

I reread the diagnosis again. What did this mean? *This isn't right. That can't be the reason.* Reece was the epitome of good health. Ray and I never had reason to think otherwise.

Reece tapped his finger on the scientific words. "I don't understand those words at the end and what they mean … actually, it doesn't matter. I'm just happy I don't measure up. They can take some other dipstick."

"It's something to do with blood clotting. Probably since birth but nothing we ever knew about or had reason to suspect. You've always been so healthy and, God forbid, never had any broken bones or even stitches." I glanced at my handsome, strong son. "How do you really feel about this, honey?"

Keeping my composure seemed as difficult as sleeping through a tornado. My mind swirled with confusion at the reason for Reece's rejection. *Calm. Stay calm.*

He leaned against the counter and grabbed a cookie from the baking sheet.

"Hey, keep your paws off, Reecie." Allie swatted him with an oversized oven mitt. "Those are for my Girl Scout troop tonight."

"You can spare some for your favorite brother." He popped another into his mouth.

"You're my only brother," Allie teased with preteen sass.

"That's even more reason to hand the cookies over." He pretended to tackle his little sister who, loving the attention, ran around the kitchen island screaming in a high-pitched voice.

"What's the commotion in here?" Ray feigned seriousness, using an ominous tone, as he entered the side door from the garage. "Hey, honey. Got home a little earlier than usual today. So glad the last surgery was canceled. I'm pooped." Propping his jacket on the back of the kitchen chair, he surveyed his family members. "And what is the occasion to have all four of us home at the same time? We can actually eat dinner together."

"Daddy, it's Wednesday," Allie said. "You know my troop meeting is tonight. Sue's mom is picking me up in half an hour."

"And those delicious smelling cookies are going with you?"

"Of course they are." Allie beamed as she slipped the remaining cookies into a Tupperware container.

"How about you, Reece. Eating dinner with us tonight?" Ray patted Reece on the shoulder that matched his own in height.

"Supposed to meet Phil and the other boys for burgers at Rickybilt on Broadway."

"Geez, those things have been around since the forties. Your mother and I used to eat those greasy things." Ray smacked his lips. "Remember those, Ess?"

I nodded, recalling our dating days and how we sneaked away at lunchtime or after a late shift when we had no other responsibilities except each other.

Ray was in a good mood, presumably relieved to be away from hospital duties for a change. "How about we go there tonight after Allie leaves for her meeting? We'd be home before she's dropped off again, right?"

Reece gave me a sideways glance, and I knew his response would not sit well with his father. Whether he could interpret my stern look or chose to ignore it, Reece replied, "Do what you want, but I'll be going with the boys. Maybe I'll see you down there." He pulled his keys from his pocket and started for the door. "Besides, I need to tell Phil about the draft-board letter. He'll be happy for me."

Ray stepped in front of his son. "Did the letter come?" The short-lived, jovial tone dissipated.

Reece gestured to the letter on the kitchen table, a sure indication he, as well as I, wasn't sure how his father would respond.

"And?" Ray grabbed for it. Except for Allie's humming, the room was silent.

Finally, Ray peered above his horn-rimmed glasses. "They don't want you over a little blood deficiency, huh?"

"Sure, they do." I tried to intercede the raw and mixed emotions that were surely churning inside my husband and dragging him back to a similar letter he'd received during World War II. "But it's against the medical guidelines if something came up in the physical." I glanced at Reece, his eyes lowered and staring at the floor. "Probably something small, a technicality."

"Then we'll have him examined again." Ray shot his son a look as if he'd cheated on a college exam. "Isn't that right, son?"

The way Reece raised his eyes and glared at his father, the Earth fell off its axis. And if the world wasn't already a mess, now it spun out of control, sending the members of the White family reeling in separate directions.

"I'm glad they don't want me!" Reece shouted. Allie dropped the baking sheet she was stowing away in the cupboard. The metal clanging on the floor syncopated with more shouts and curse words from my husband and son.

"I've been worried sick about you going, but it's no excuse not to want to defend your country." Ray batted a kitchen chair to the side, and at the same time, Reece bent down to retrieve the cookie sheet. The chair and Reece's nose collided, and blood spewed on to the kitchen floor.

"For heaven's sake, Ray. Look what you've done." I grabbed a dishrag and tried to wipe Reece's face. But he grabbed it from my hand and held it under his nose—the white dishcloth turning red.

"Daddy, you hurt him!" Allie screamed. "Reecie, you got blood all over your face!"

"I'm all right"—Reece glared at his sister—"and quit being such a baby."

Allie burst into tears and ran down the hallway to her bedroom.

"So this is all my fault?" Ray slumped into a chair, defeated by a system that had denied his dream years ago, and now repeated the offense on his son.

"Dad, I don't understand why I failed the physical." Reece paused, trying to calm his shaky voice. "Sure, I'm strong, fast, smart … all the reasons why the military would want to send me off to fight their war." He stepped toward his father, and Ray stood, meeting him face-to-face. "But I don't care what they want or what they need. The way I see it, I literally dodged a bullet and can have a long, happy life."

For too long, the two men I loved most, locked eyes as if in a mental tug-of-war.

Ray broke the silence and spoke first. "I love you, Reece, and more than anything, I want you to have a good life. But why the physicians, or maybe it was the draft board"—he shook his head—"why they stripped you of the honor and every good American's dream to serve—"

"It's your dream, Dad, not mine." As if Reece had raised a gun to his father, Ray froze. "And if you really loved me, you wouldn't want me to die at the expense of your own unrealized, patriotic duty."

The proverbial bullet lodged in Ray's heart. He stumbled back against the wall as Reece charged toward the garage door.

"Honey, don't leave like this. Your nose is still bleeding. There must be something to what they found in your physical. Let me help you clean up." I reached for his shirtsleeve, but he pulled away.

"Then don't do this, Mom." Like a teenager, his voice cracked, but he and I knew the subject of the evening's argument was reserved only for a man.

"I'll be home late."

The door shut behind him, and I turned to see Ray faltering down the hallway as if he had aged a hundred years.

* * * * *

Why now? Almost forty years later. The sands of my time were nearly spent. My secret had been buried for so long, it didn't need to be exposed. It was intended to be taken to the grave—to eventually disintegrate and disappear—the rotten thing I had done. Only God knew my sin.

But now the wind swept off the ocean, blowing my hair across my face. The foreboding water had more to say. I wrapped my sweater tighter, preparing myself for the images that refused to go away.

* * * * *

Sleep didn't come easily that night for Ray or me. We'd tossed and turned, both of us glancing at the glowing clock on the dresser across the room.

At 1:22 a.m., I was jostled from sleep that had finally come. Ray's side of the bed was empty. Probably in the bathroom. At the sound of voices down the hallway, I slid out of bed and wrapped myself in my robe.

When my eyes adjusted to the dim light, Ray stood with his back to me in the foyer. Across from him, hats in hands and heads shaking, were two policemen.

"What's wrong, officers?" I sidled next to my husband, threading my arm under his.

Neither answered at first, but eyes darted between Ray and me. "Ma'am," the younger one spoke, "I—"

"Essie … Reece was in an accident. He and Phil were out driving and …"

My legs began to give way, and I grabbed Ray. "Is he at the hospital? Hurry, let's—"

Ray clung to my arm as I started to pull away. The white-faced, contorted expression on my husband's face terrified me.

"Well, what are we waiting for, Ray?"

"He's dead, Essie," he whispered. Each word pierced my heart like a knife.

Then, as an explosion, its sound traveling through space, each syllable reverberated at decibels beyond human measure. I covered my ears and screamed, "No!"

Wrapping me in his arms, Ray squeezed so tightly I couldn't catch my breath. And then it didn't matter. *Please, God … let me die.*

"Dear God. Oh, Essie. I'm so sorry. What did I do?" Ray's body wracked with sobs, heaving uncontrollably on top of mine, until he released me, his arms limp at his sides.

"Mr. and Mrs. White, if there's anything we can do …" The older officer wiped his eyes with the back of his hand. "I have kids of my own, and … this is the hardest part of the job."

"Could it be a mistake?" Pleading with him for a reprise, I offered shaky hands. He held them in both of his hands and shook his head.

"We have the driver's licenses of both young men."

"Phil?" I gasped. To this point, I'd only thought of my own child, as a parent is allowed to do. "Is he all right?"

"Both are deceased. Most likely killed on impact. They were going at a high speed around the tight corner on Ridge Road before hitting the tree. The way the skid marks measured, there wasn't much time for him to stop."

Anger slithered from my mouth. "We never should have let him go driving with that irresponsible Phil … in that fast car of his." I looked to Ray for support, but he was in a fog, lost somewhere where torturous thoughts were served out in droves.

"Ma'am"—the officer's hat twisted in his hands—"your son was driving." The serpent that had slithered from my throat reeled around, striking and injecting its poison into my veins.

"I see." The response was barely audible. Again, I slipped my arm beneath Ray's as we thanked the officers for their service and closed the door. Somewhere a few neighborhoods away, I imagined another mother and father were doing the same, and for them, my heart broke a thousand times over again.

* * * * *

"Ma'am? Are you okay?" Startled, I turned my tearstained face toward the voice.

"Sorry if I scared you, but I was un-stacking the chairs before the early birds flock the beach, and I heard you crying."

The young man, probably in his late teens, was dressed in white— T-shirt and pants, even a white ball cap. For a moment, I could have mistaken him for an angel, except for the resort logo stitched on the front pocket.

"No … I mean, yes, I'm fine." I smoothed my windblown hair. "Suppose I was having a senior moment."

"Oh, one of those." Even in the dim light, when he smiled his teeth were bright white against his tan skin. "My grandparents joke about that." He tilted his head. "But I thought that's when you can't remember something."

I stared at the handsome boy, who cruelly and yet beautifully, resembled Reece—the tall and lanky build of a boy soon to become a man and the lopsided smile, assuring that life was all okay.

"That's what some might say." I wobbled to a stand and thanked him for caring.

"You have a nice day, ma'am." He gave a quick wave as he headed to the next stack of chairs. "Impossible not to when you're in paradise."

Chapter Twenty-Nine

Essie ~ Painted Memories

Just as Lou had faked a bellyache on our first dinner date, now it was my turn. Montezuma's Revenge was an easy scapegoat and gave me an excuse for avoiding dates, outings, or lengthy phone calls once we'd returned to Colorado. There was plenty to think about and sort through—ghosts from my past had returned, and they were not friendly.

* * * * *

Intuition and past experience dictated my next move. Time in my basement art room. That's what I used to do when I needed clarity and calm. That's what I needed now. Perhaps my long-neglected art materials could mix up a palette of wisdom as to my future, with or without Lou.

My studio, as I preferred to call it, consisted of a rickety easel and a thrift-store vanity. I'd painted each drawer a different color and stuffed them with paint tubes, brushes, paint-stained water bowls, and clippings from the newspaper and magazines of local art shows, pretty landscapes, and anything else that might inspire my own art. A gooseneck lamp provided enough illumination, but nothing compared to natural light.

Maybe today I'd haul my supplies upstairs and set up in the kitchen where the morning sun shone brightest. Besides, I'd most likely be eating my meals alone for the rest of my life, or at least until Allie sent me away to some *home*. I grinned. No, I'd become an eccentric artist, holed up in my kitchen studio with twenty cats, although I prefer dogs, and paint in my pajamas.

I was surprised when I heard Allie call my name from the top of the stairs.

"Yes, I'm down here." I pushed a box aside with my foot and set another on the Ping-Pong table that hadn't been used since the kids were teenagers. "I didn't know you were stopping by."

Footsteps trotted down the stairs, and then there was Allie—hands on hips and lips pursed. For a moment, I felt as if I'd been caught doing something naughty—like when I caught Reece smoking cigarettes with his high school buddy or Allie and the boy next door playing Spin the Bottle.

"What in the world are you doing down here?" Her voice was stern. Now I really felt convicted of ... something.

"First, are you sick?"

"No. I'm feeling fine. Why?"

"Well, I ran into a certain gentleman at the grocery store, and he informed me you've been too ill to see him. So sick that you aren't returning calls. He's worried about you." She shook her head slowly. "And he mentioned something—"

"Ever since our trip, my stomach has been out of whack. You know what they say about drinking the water in Mexico."

Allie stepped closer, and the three inches she had on my five-foot-three stature felt monumental.

"Lou asked you to marry him. You didn't even tell me, and now you won't talk to him?" Allie half talked, half shrieked. "I'm all for happily ever after, but it'd be nice to know what's going on." She lapped once around the Ping-Pong table and then faced me again. "I felt like an idiot when he told me he proposed. He figured I knew all about it."

"You make me sound like I'm about to elope, or I'm the world's worst heartbreaker. Besides, I wouldn't call it a full proposal. We're in the discussion phase."

"Even though you won't talk to him? And that would be the world's *best* heartbreaker." Allie pressed her palms on to the dusty table. "He said the last time you talked, you'd even bailed out on going to church. You never do that."

"These sure dry out." I tossed a dried tube of paint in the wastebasket.

"Don't change the subject. Anyway, the paint's gone bad more likely because you haven't painted in years."

"I've dabbled, but not much."

"And from past observation, you paint when you're upset."

"And how would you know that?" I lifted a brush and ran my fingers through the soft bristles.

"Because it's the same with my writing. I meet deadlines when I have to, but it's those melancholy, even hard times when I have to write just like I have to breathe." She lifted a brush and swiped it across her palm. "I bet you are, or at least used to be, that way with your painting."

"Probably some truth to that."

I sighed, allowing her words to sink in.

"When your father was sick, I tried to paint late at night when it was hard to sleep because of worrying about him. I don't think I had the energy. After he passed away, I thought I'd begin painting again to keep me company when all I wanted was to be with him. But I picked up my brush only a time or two."

"But you really stopped painting after Reece died."

An elephant may as well have walked into the room, but I avoided my daughter's comment and continued to tidy my art supplies. No doubt, there was validity to what Allie said. Painting was my escape when the kids were young and later became busy teenagers, consumed with their own lives. When life threw challenges and tragedies my way, art seemed to call to me like a siren. But when Reece died, I refused to allow myself to retreat behind layers of paint and into imaginary places. I no longer deserved such a gift.

"So, what's bothering you?" She closed the next drawer I was about to tackle. "Are you nervous about getting married? Is he pressuring you?"

"Heaven's no," I spoke hastily. "Neither of us is in a big hurry. We simply talked at length about it and decided that's what we'd like, eventually."

"Mom, *eventually* takes on its own meaning when neither of you are spring chickens."

"I realize that. If we marry, it'll be because we love one another and make each other's life more complete."

"Well, that's beautiful, and you have my blessing if you decide to marry. Besides, Lou makes me laugh, and that's always good."

"I agree. If things go that way, I'm glad I have your support, and we'll have a comedian in the family." I feigned a smile. "Maybe it's only the jitters. Getting hitched is a big decision, especially at my age."

"True. But remember what you said. Love knows no age."

I lifted an unfinished painting of crocuses emerging from the snow. I'd begun the piece shortly after Ray died, but abandoned it when I felt too hopeless to add the beautiful hues of purple in stark contrast to the whites and grays of snow. Now, as if the chill had returned, I felt frozen in my emotions, only a lingering hopelessness for what I had done.

I forced myself to look at Allie. The concern on her face was evident. *Better to get out of the basement and into the sunshine.* "How about I leave the rest of this mess for another day when you have time to help? You're a much better organizer and can purge while I supervise." I surveyed the piles of unused household items that migrate to the basement. "There's more in the closet that I can't even begin to think about. Old Christmas crafts, unfinished cross-stitching, sections of quilts—all those projects that seemed so important at the time—stuffed into boxes." I shut the closet door. "Your old Girl Scout sewing projects are in there too."

"Oh my gosh. I haven't thought about those forever." Allie pushed by me and opened the door. "Give me a sec. I just have to take a peek."

She removed box after box from the shelves, creating a bigger mess than when I started. Tired and cranky, I sank into a long-forgotten chair and watched. For Allie, digging into her past was exciting, a treasure hunt for inconspicuous items and memories of childhood times.

For me—even though there were joyous times like marrying Ray and the birth of our children—an archaeological trek into my past was mired in grief, sadness, and guilt. And as I contemplated a future with Lou, the man who had bared his soul and come clean with his past, guilt rose up and covered me like a dense and unbreakable fog.

As I watched Allie hold up a wrinkled, gingham apron, overbearing questions pummeled my mind. Could I continue the charade to bury my past and still be able to laugh with family and friends, commune and pray at church, and love Lou to the extent he deserved to be loved? Most importantly, could I look at myself in the mirror?

"Mom, what's this?" Allie was crouched on her knees, her back to me. "It's familiar, but I can't place it."

"Let me see." I pushed myself from the chair and looked over her shoulder. My heart skipped a beat as my hand went to my mouth.

"This is such a strange painting," Allie mused. "It's kind of like one that hung over the fireplace when I was a kid. You were so proud when you brought that one home from your art class. I remember Dad drilled a hole into the brick and strung a wire to hold it in place."

"In that portrait class, I learned to draw and paint people." My voice was robotic, remembering what I'd done to the painting shortly after

Reece was killed. "I painted it from a Polaroid I'd brought to class. Our neighbor, Mr. Steward, had taken the photo of us with his new camera."

Allie spun around. "Mom, this is the same painting." She stared at me with wild eyes. "What happened to it? It used to be a painting of our whole family. All of us on the front porch."

Blood seemed to drain from me as my jaw tightened and my lips quivered. I looked at Allie and back at the painting. Two of the four people had been painted over in a hazy sort of wash, features barely discernable as though they had been erased from time.

"Why did you paint over you and Reece? Why did you destroy our beautiful family?"

My legs weakened, and I grabbed for the door jam.

"Mom, you okay?" Allie jumped to her feet and steadied my arm. "Maybe you really are sick."

I shook my head and motioned to the stairwell. I needed fresh air, but more importantly, it was my turn to ask Allie to join me for an important meeting. Tomorrow. I'd ask her to come back tomorrow. The topic would be difficult and lopsided, one that a mother should never have to have with her daughter. Regardless, I needed to come clean with someone, a best friend, the person who knew me best, and of course, that was Allie.

That night, as I lay awake in bed contemplating how the next day would play out, darkness weighed on me. Was this what it was like to lie in the grave, devoid of light, unable to see, and restless? Suffocating as each shovelful of guilt was thrown on top of me? Allie's question echoed in my mind: *Why did you destroy our beautiful family?*

Chapter Thirty

When Allie arrived and I unlocked the door to let her in, her deadpan expression meant she had not come over for light conversation. For this *very* important meeting, I'm sure she was convinced that I was the one with relationship troubles.

With the coffee and tea brewed, a plate of toast and jam prepared, and a bowl of berries rinsed, I ushered her into the kitchen and motioned to the table. Over the years, the kitchen table was privy to many family talks, late-night discussions, plenty of celebrations, and sometimes fights. Now, I wondered how vividly she recalled the night her brother stormed out … the last time we saw Reece alive.

"I admit, Mom, you have me worried." Allie shifted in her chair and poked at a raspberry. "You're acting kind of strange lately."

I almost spoke in defense of myself, but I paused. This was what I needed to do.

I breathed deeply and then, figuratively, jumped off the cliff.

"Allie, I have something very difficult to tell you, and I need you to hear me out. Let me tell you the whole story, and then we can talk."

"Oh Mom, you have cancer!" She lunged across the table and grabbed my hands.

"No! I most certainly do not." I squeezed her hands and gently pushed them back to her side of the expanse. "Nothing's wrong with me, and I'm sorry I didn't make that clear up front."

"Well, don't ever scare me like that again. Geez." She slumped in her chair and crossed her arms. "Okay, the suspense is killing me."

I didn't intend to play on what she said, but the words spilled out. "I killed your brother."

Allie's mouth gaped before she sputtered a response. "What? What did you say?"

"I mean … I didn't … my actions … something I did … or didn't do … was ultimately responsible for Reece dying." My mouth went dry, and I steadied the teacup with both hands.

"Mom"—Allie's face was contorted—"you aren't making any sense at all."

I set my cup on the table and folded my hands in a silent prayer. *Dear Lord, help me tell the truth, and don't let Allie hate me.* "I need you to listen now."

She sat still as I stepped back in time, when Reece was still alive, as if navigating a field of land mines.

✳ ✳ ✳ ✳ ✳

February 16, 1968

"I'm off to work, Ray," I called from the front door. "Will you be home in time for dinner?"

My husband, still in his pajamas, had followed me into the foyer, coffee mug in hand. "Thought you didn't have a shift today."

"Covering for a new gal. Already calling in sick, can you believe it?"

"Where's the work ethic?" He pecked me on the cheek. "I've got the late one, so no, won't make it home for dinner. Save me something to eat if Reece doesn't devour it all."

"Should be home by five." I scooted down the walk to my car and slipped inside. *Why was it so easy to lie to him?* There was no shift to cover for an imaginary, irresponsible nurse. I'd traded workdays with Betsy as soon as the plan formulated in my mind. I needed to be working at the hospital on February sixteenth, the appointed date for Reece's draft physical.

The waiting room was already crowded by eight o'clock, filled with young men, most recently turned eighteen and sprouting facial hair. Each physical examination took less than an hour. The hospital staff had the system down to a science since the war had been drawing more and more soon-to-be soldiers in droves.

My assignment for the day was down the hall in pediatrics, but I'd share the same nursing station with the staff helping with the military physicals. As I read the notes from last night's shift nurses, my hands trembled, the clipboard shaking in unison. *This is the easy part,* I reminded myself.

At a quarter to nine, I casually passed by the waiting room, expecting to see Reece in the queue for his exam. Some of the young men were slumped forward, elbows on knees, and staring at the floor. Others paced the rows between the vinyl-clad chairs, either trying to calm their fears of what lay ahead or anxiously awaiting a clean bill of health and eager to serve the country. *Maybe he chose not to come, hoping for the slim chance the government would pass over him—disregard the fact his number had been called.*

"Hey, Mom." Reece's low voice startled me. "Looking for someone?"

"Oh, hi, honey." I forced a smile. "Figured you'd already be here."

"A party I would have preferred to miss." He ran his fingers through his thick hair, a gesture he'd done ever since he was two, when his hair had grown long enough to notice. "But Dad and I had a good talk last night after you went to sleep. He said the war is winding down, and the Army may not need too many more troops anyway."

Talk of the war subsiding had bubbled on and off the news, but like champagne released, the fizz dissipated quickly, and the excitement disappeared by the following days' reports.

"That's what we can pray for."

"Besides, he said there's plenty of non-combat assignments." He revealed a white-toothed grin. "I can make a mean grilled cheese sandwich. Maybe they'll let me be a cook. Soldiers have to eat, right?"

I wanted to brainstorm with my son all the possible jobs that would keep him out of imminent danger, but the registration nurse called his name. *Yes, his name is on the list and won't be erased or overlooked because his mother can't bear the reality of letting him go.*

"I'd stop and say goodbye when I'm finished, but Phil's meeting me to work on the brakes of his new Chevy." As he started toward the check-in desk, he called back over his shoulder, "His number hasn't been called yet, so he's planning on having the time of his life for now."

* * * * *

My second lie of the day would be much more difficult. The time on the wall clock was ten twenty. Clipboards laden with paperwork already lined the desk area from the earliest appointments. Several white-coated doctors hovered over the piles, flipping through reports of blood profiles and physical exam observations and measurements, scrawling illegible signatures on dotted lines.

Illegible. Like cracking a cheesy case on *Dragnet,* I knew what to do. But in this case, I would be the criminal. For what needed to be done, my sentence would be real if caught—not played out on some Hollywood set where I'd leave for the day and enjoy a martini over dinner. A good part of my life, and maybe Reece's, would be spent behind bars.

Doris, a nurse who shared the same duties as I, waddled toward the station with an armload of files. "Didn't know your son was coming in today. I haven't seen him in years, but I noticed his name right away." The papers began to topple, and I helped stabilize the pile. "He sure is a handsome boy. Wish we could set him up with one of my daughters. Kathleen's a senior this year at East, and I'm sure she'd love—"

She stopped mid-sentence, and her face reddened. I understood.

"I'm sorry, Essie. That was insensitive." She stepped around me and balanced the papers on the countertop. "I better get back there. Full house today."

With my eyes on Doris, my thoughts focused on the mound of papers to my right. *Reece's records have to be in there.*

Quickly, I sorted the manila folders into stacks per attending physician while scanning the neatly printed, patient's last name, then first, on the protruding tab. Nearly halfway through the pile, WHITE, REECE surfaced. Two doctors, along with a flustered nurse, conversed on the other side of the nurse's station. Doctor Evans, one of the newer physicians on staff, wasn't in sight.

If someone walks by, they won't notice whose papers I'm reading if my hand covers the tab. Since I was sure Reece would pass his exam with an A+, the scenario of what ailment, one severe enough to cause the military to doubt his ability to serve in combat, had played out in my mind since the draft letter had arrived. Now, like a thief against an impending alarm, I had to act quickly and decide what result could be changed … or added. Altered blood pressure and heart rate could easily be checked again. Blood results were still blank, awaiting results from the lab. Reflexes, vision, and hearing were perfect. My heart raced as I tried to suppress the urge to panic.

"Hey, Essie." A sweet voice next to me caught me off guard. "I'm in PDs today."

On point, I closed the folder and slipped it under the other files. "Oh, hi, Tracy." Despite the controlled, cool temperature in the hospital, my face burned, assuring my face had reddened.

"You okay? Look a little off." She tilted her head to the side as if taking my temperature through mind reading.

"I'm fine. Probably one of those darn hot flashes that keep sneaking up on me." *There, that was convincing.* "I really need to get some work—"

"I keep hearing about those dreaded things." Tracy shook her head, her ponytail sweeping back and forth on her shoulders. "Glad I'm not there yet."

"Enjoy it while you can." I feigned reading the wall chart of room assignments, hoping she'd be on her way and I could return to the task at hand.

"Oh, Essie. It's so awful." Her eyes widened. "They usually have me up on the surgery floor, but I'm covering for Nurse Caldwell. You know her, don't you?"

I raised my head. "Sure do. Is she okay?"

"She and her husband got word last night their son's been killed. I don't know the details, but something about him stepping on a mine." Her arms hung limply at her sides. "I've been praying he didn't have a chance to know what happened."

My head swirled and I grasped the counter. "You're right, Tracy, I'm not feeling well." Deftly, I lifted the pile of papers and held them to my chest. "Doctor Evans needs these, then I'll rest for a few minutes in the break room."

Before Tracy could help, I half-jogged down the hallway. The hospital was crammed with activity—orderlies pushing carts, nurses rushing with hands full of supplies and paperwork, and doctors ducking in and out of patient rooms.

I paused outside the restroom, momentarily frozen before pushing the door open with my shoulder and slipping inside. I leaned against the wall and panted. Like a good Boy Scout, a nurse is always prepared. With barely a free hand, I unclipped the pen from my front pocket, lifted the bottom file, and flipped the pages to Reece's medical history.

Hesitation whispered in my ear before I set the pen to paper. *This isn't right. You shouldn't meddle with fate.*

But the news of the Caldwell boy—most likely a red-headed, freckled version of his mother—flashed across my mind like a film reel breaking in mid movie, tossing disjointed images across the screen before the theater goes dark.

With a nearly illegible doctor's scrawl, I scribbled, Traumatic head injury—forehead contusion and laceration, 3/22/66.

Then, like floodlights being switched on, the restroom door opened, and Tracy stepped inside.

"Essie, you look even worse. I couldn't let you run off like that. I saw you go in the bathroom and figured you had to vomit or something." She extended her arms. "Here, I'll take those to Doc Evans. He's waiting at the station." She lifted the files and held them tightly. "You, my dear"—she patted my shaking arm—"need to ask permission to go home. We don't need any sick nurses around this place."

As the door swung shut behind the young nurse, I was motionless except for my racing heart. My plan was nearly foiled. I could do nothing more to save my son. Before leaving the bathroom, I stared at my disheveled reflection looking back at me. Although the woman in the mirror knew my motive, she showed no emotion—her face blank—as if she, too, was willing to take our secret to the grave.

* * * * *

"I lied, Allie. I lied about a medical condition Reece never had, and after that, everything spiraled out of control." I drooped over the table, spent from retracing the steps of my deception.

"But Reece wrecked Dad's car in the school parking lot his sophomore year right after getting his license." Allie shook her head. "Dad was fuming when he found out the front bumper of the Buick was bashed in."

"Yes, but Reece had only a small cut … didn't need stitches and only left a small scar. No head injury. Nothing serious."

I'm not sure how I expected Allie to respond, but her blank stare pushed me to tell more.

"Honey, do you remember an argument between your father and brother? In this kitchen, the night Reece left?"

As if subconsciously, Allie slowly lifted her hand and brushed it across her nose. "I'll never forget it. There was blood all over Reece's face. Scared me to death. I ran to my room."

"Yes," I whispered, recalling that maternal tug-of-war of which child to attend to first. "It was an accident. Ray didn't mean to hit him with the chair. Everything that night happened so fast."

Neither of us spoke. Despite Ray and I eventually updating much of the kitchen once Allie was grown and on her own—new flooring, replacing appliances and countertops, and repainting the brown cabinets to white, every detail of the night was precise.

"Why didn't you and Dad ever move?" She must have been replaying the same horror film in her mind. "Get away from this house and the bad memories?"

It was a fair question, and I needed to give my answer time to collect. I pushed from the table and looked out the window. Ray was a good husband and father, a well-respected and hard-working man. He loved me and was crazy about his kids. I never doubted that. But he carried a bitter root.

When Ray wasn't making his rounds or performing surgery at the hospital, he was often exhausted, planted in front of the television watching the ABC Evening News with anchorman, Frank Reynolds, hanging on to every commentary and image of the war in the jungles of Vietnam and Cambodia.

"Gotta love that man," he said each evening. As I continued looking out the window, it was as if I could still hear Ray's voice. "Infantry Army Sergeant, received the Purple Heart ... now serving his country on the evening news. He'd probably still be out in the field if the military hadn't retired him."

My husband's patriotism was commendable, but for him, not being able to serve in the military due to flat feet had been a thorn in his side, even after World War II ended. Although his medical skills eventually became invaluable stateside when soldiers arrived home from the Korean and early Vietnam wars, we never spoke about him being denied the same heroic role. I knew the void had allowed an emotional wound to fester, eating away at his patriotic core and testing our marital bliss.

Allie's terse voice yanked me back to the gray granite versus green laminate counter-topped kitchen.

"Did Dad know what you did?"

"No." That answer was definitive. "I never told him."

"Why not?"

"It would have crushed him ... and he would have hated me." I hung my head. "We agreed on most things, but not the war. Ray was a keen debater and extremely passionate about controversial topics, especially whether our troops should be in the war."

"Strong opinions about most things, that was for sure," Allie added. "Took him a while to warm up to the fact I wasn't marrying a good ole American boy."

"Your father loved Peter."

"Eventually."

I bobbed my head in agreement.

"After some heated arguments, I'd surrendered, at least outwardly. My best defense was a small section of Scripture highlighted in my Bible, Hebrews 12:14–15. I read it often. 'Make every effort to live in peace with everyone and to be holy; without holiness no one will see the Lord. See to it that no one falls short of the grace of God, and that no bitter root grows up to cause trouble and defile many.' I'm surprised I can still recite it."

As though needing to digest all that she had heard, Allie stood and paced the kitchen. "But I don't understand." She stopped and glared at me with challenging eyes. "You falsified a report about Reece's health so he wouldn't have to go to war. You never told Dad what you did. But it didn't matter. The doctors found something anyway, something bad enough that he couldn't serve."

Her voice escalated with each accusation until she was nearly shouting. I remained silent, deserving her rage.

"Then the Army denied Reece, and Dad freaked out based on his own past issues … and the whole family got in some stupid fight that night, and Reece ran out and rammed himself and his best friend into a tree?" With her last words barely set free, she broke down and wept.

I stood frozen with my hand covering my mouth. My own tears, which should have come, were non-existent—perhaps cried too many times that my sorrow had turned to bitter root.

When she gathered herself and finally spoke, her next words brought me to my knees. "And after all these years, you know what I've done, Mom?"

I shook my head.

"I've blamed myself for screaming and crying, getting everyone even more upset. If I hadn't run away to my room, I could have stopped Reece." She was sobbing now, words coming out in bits and pieces. "He would have listened … to me. He loved … me … but he … slammed the car into that …"

"Oh, Allie." My chest tightened. "It was never your fault. It was all mine. Even though the doctors found something else, I was determined to take my chances and change an outcome. That letter just as easily could have stated my reason for the rejection, and that night would have had the same horrific outcome.

"So why did you think you were entitled … that you had the right to mess with fate?"

My hand slowly fell away from my mouth as I uttered the truth, "To save my son's life."

* * * * *

I knew it was best I had told Allie the truth. Methodically, she had gathered her purse and keys, poured a coffee-to-go, mentioned she'd talk with me later, and driven away.

That day, I'd lifted my phone several times to call her. But I didn't know what to say. Plus, she deserved time to be alone with her thoughts, maybe share my dubious past with Peter, and allow the last thirty-eight years to catch up to her.

I rolled to one side of my bed and flicked on the lamp. Tonight, the light would remain on. First thing in the morning, I'd call Lou and insist that he come for breakfast when the confession of a sinner would be shared once again.

Chapter Thirty-One

Allie ~ Plot Twist

My computer and I are usually best of friends. Today, and maybe forever, we might as well call this relationship quits and part ways. The blank word document says it all. I've nothing to say.

"Hey, babe." Peter's fingers kneaded my hunched shoulders. "Wow, you're super tight. What's up with that?"

"Nothing makes sense lately." I sighed.

"Your new book?"

"Yeah, this book, the next one … my mom. She's acting super odd … shared some hard things with me this morning. And, get this, didn't tell me Lou proposed to her in Mexico, and yet now she's avoiding him."

"Maybe she's nervous. But, I bet just like in your stories, love will prevail." With his customary gesture when I was writing, Peter kissed me on top of my head.

"Ah, like the title of my debut novel. Good ole *Love Will Prevail.*" I turned and faced my husband. "I was so naïve." The deep blue eyes and thick eyelashes caught my attention years ago and held me captive. But lately, perhaps from the unknown … or a genuine fear … an unwelcomed urge to flee came over me.

He grabbed my hips and pulled me closer. "I liked that one. Steamy scenes and lots of—"

"Messed up relationships." I stepped back. "Peter, I thought I had this whole love thing figured out, but I don't. Not even close. The whole dating online for Mom was a mistake. Sure, Lou is a great guy and makes her laugh. They have a lot of fun together, and that's all good."

"And what's wrong with that? She seems happy, and why not let her enjoy life with someone who cares about her after being such a good wife to your dad for so many years? She deserves it."

"Does she?" I was shocked by my quick response, and by Peter's raised brows, he was surprised as well.

He extended his hands toward mine, and, hesitantly, I offered mine. After all, I had just betrayed my own mother. *What kind of person does that make me?*

I led Peter to the sofa and filled him in about the exchange that occurred with Mom a few hours earlier. I spoke and wept, and he listened—another attribute about him that drew me in from the start of our relationship. As he held me and offered a clean tissue, I was reminded again that too much time slipped away as my writing and his work tipped the scales in their favor instead of ours.

"So, where does this leave you and your mom?" He leaned back and crossed his arms, and in his pragmatic manner asked, "What are you going to do with this revelation about the past?"

I slouched into the pillows and wondered the same. After staring at the ceiling for too long, I whispered, "Try to let it go … I mean, I'll always think about my brother and the last time I saw him. Mom said the horrible accident wasn't my fault, and I want to believe that." I blinked away more tears. "It wasn't her fault either."

I stood slowly, feeling as though I'd aged in a matter of hours. "Strange how the past makes us revisit and hang out there for a while. Then, as if it's had enough of the memories, laments and regrets, it says, 'Hey, get out of here! Time to leave. Move forward to the present … and maybe if you don't screw up, a bright future might lie ahead.'"

"I understand." Peter let out a long exhale, as though propelling himself away from the past. "Although nothing like your family's tragedy happened to me, I do look back and wonder what could have been if decisions and actions had been different."

"Like not leaving Paris?" My eyes met his, and I imagined he was envisioning his beautiful hometown.

"I suppose, but then I never would have met you." He held my hand. "Allie, for the most part, we'll never know the outcome from one small turn, the timing of our movements … being early or late." He glanced at his watch. "Darn! And I'm going to be late for an appointment."

"I thought you didn't go in until the afternoon today." I feigned a pout, but this time, I felt emptiness at the mention of him rushing off to work again. My emotions and heart were still on shaky ground, and

I needed his steadiness to anchor me.

"Yeah, I have the two to nine shift, but I have a lunch meeting first." He nearly jumped from the sofa, and I followed after him toward the coat closet.

Before I could lasso my thought, words slipped out. "Are you having an affair?"

As though he'd run into an invisible wall, Peter stopped and reeled around. "Are you kidding? Hon, that's ridic—"

"Maggie. The one who's worked at the bookstore in the mall for years."

"You're nuts." He rolled his eyes so dramatically they could have spun from his head. "A woman who only speaks in Old English Dictionary vocab and resembles Ichabod Crane? If I'm attracted to her, then I am in worse shape than I ever imagined."

He shot me a sideways look, and I wondered if there was truth to what he said … maybe I am nuts.

Although he attempted humor, his response was mixed with a glare. "Besides, Maggie is old, perhaps an ancient relic escaped from the museum and feigning as a store clerk to research modern-day culture." He tugged on his jacket and opened the front door. "Allie, clearly, your imagination is alive and well. You shouldn't have any trouble getting back into your writing while I'm working … and I emphasize, *working*."

Apparently, I was good at blurting out—a habit even my elementary teachers confirmed—so why stop now?

"Maggie told me about the other woman." *There, I picked up the rock and threw it, hitting dead center.*

Peter slammed the door and spun around with hands on his hips. "Allie," he said nodding toward the living room, "back to the sofa."

Reminiscent of a trip to the principal's office after I'd punched a girl on the playground for calling my best friend bad names, I dragged my feet toward the sofa. But I had plenty to say to my husband. For all I knew, our marriage was falling apart. Bad things in relationships didn't happen only in my novels.

This time we sat on opposite ends of the sofa, me staring at my Birkenstocks and he, most likely, still glaring.

"*Je ne peux pas y croire.*"

When Peter speaks French, even if I don't know what he's saying, he gets my attention.

"Whatever you do, don't say something I can't understand."

"Then, I'll translate ... I can't believe it." His shoulders slumped. "Allie, why in the world would you accuse me of having an affair?"

"I didn't accuse you. I asked. Besides, to refresh your memory, you questioned my faithfulness not too long ago."

"That was about your obsessive writing, not a real person." He stood, making our sofa time extra brief.

"Then I'll quit writing. No more Allie the author." I stood as well, trying to make myself feel matched to his five-foot-eleven stature. "Maybe I'm not so great at it anyway."

"You know that's not true. You're extremely talented. We agreed your writing is a part of you—just not night and day."

"Right, this is about you right now."

"Then talk away." He brushed his hand in the air. "I'm curious to know exactly what I've done that's so wrong."

I resumed my cross-legged position on the sofa. *Better to be grounded to venture into this territory.* "Maggie was edgy when I stopped in the store to sign copies of my new book."

"Isn't she always?" he asked.

"Yes, but even more than usual. After I did the signings, she led me behind the Cooking and Lifestyle shelf ... said she had some news to share."

"And?"

"She felt obligated as a fellow book lover and writer—although she kept confessing that she wasn't published, like she had committed some sort of horrific crime and needed to apologize. Anyway, she felt she had to tell me she'd seen you having coffee with a younger, and, of course, attractive woman in the food court."

"Isn't the man allowed to drink?"

"I even said that and added the woman was probably interviewing with you."

"Very possible. I interview plenty of salesclerks, and it's a little awkward to meet between Vince Camuto and Steve Madden."

I returned a hard smile to his attempt to lighten the topic with a play on shoe brands.

"I'd like to think that, but ..." my fingers fidgeted with the pillow fringe. "Maggie said she's seen you with her on more than one occasion having more than coffee. You've been eating lunch together in the food court, even Pizza Hut. That's kind of like a dinner."

"It's Tracy Ringold. Now this makes sense." Peter rubbed his temple, and I hoped another migraine wasn't lurking nearby—ready to pounce when stress was on the rise. "We've been having meetings in the food court over the last several weeks. She's the corporate manager, and we've been discussing the transition plan—"

"You've been fired?"

"Of course not! I'm getting accused of everything. Geez, babe, I wish you would have brought this up sooner and told Maggie to mind her own business …" He looked at me with sad eyes. "Or better yet, I wish you would trust me." He took my hands and pressed my fingers to his lips. "Allie, je *t'aime pour toujours*."

I listened to his words and breathed in their truth. "Now, that is French I'll never tire of hearing … and I understand every word. I love you forever too." It felt right to kiss him … my Frenchman … my husband.

"Now, explain to me about this transition," I said.

"Well, I suppose I should have brought that up sooner as well." A flush crept across his face. "I didn't want to mention anything until it became a real possibility." Again, he gestured to the sofa. "*Mon cherie*, now I need to do the talking."

"What about your lunch meeting?" My eyebrows rose.

"Too late for that." He pushed my ponytail to the side and nuzzled my neck. "But never too late for us."

Chapter Thirty-Two

Lou ~ Dropping the Bomb

Hearing Essie's story felt like a bullet to the chest. My son had followed the rules, gone to war, done his patriotic duty, only to return home in a box. Now, the woman I loved revealed she was capable of the unthinkable—committing a crime to save her son's life while others were losing theirs. And just as convicting, as though I stood before the ultimate Judge with the same intention, *would I have attempted to protect my son had I known for certain that he would die if I didn't?*

I recall how stoic she was at first, pushing untouched scrambled eggs and cold toast around her plate with the tip of a fork. As her past unfolded, my food cooled—my appetite lost as I processed what she shared. She too had tried to alter the course of another, and despite her best intentions, the outcome was tragic. Like two old fools at a sappy movie, we wept for each other and for ourselves.

More than once, I pulled a wadded kerchief from my back pocket and wiped my eyes. "Essie, I don't know what to say."

"Nothing is expected," she replied. "Allie didn't know how to respond either. Yesterday, when I told her the truth, she cried. Then she got mad and left. Didn't even say goodbye." Essie blotted her eyes. "Not that I could blame her."

"She's confused. You dredged up parts of the past she'd like to forget."

"I wish I could forget." A grave expression covered Essie's face. "Like your admission at the ocean … I couldn't hide from mine any longer. When Allie found a family portrait, a picture I'd painted years ago, a heavy curtain was pulled apart, and there I was, center stage … all by myself and no place to go.

Even though my heart was forever damaged by my own son's loss, now it broke for Essie. The confession depleted her. While she spilled out her past wrongs across the kitchen table, she seemed to wilt—a vibrant flower slowly dying.

With elbows propped and chin on folded hands, she whispered, "Whatever is the outcome, for us, for me … the bomb's dropped, and the fallout will be what it will be."

"Sounds like something I would say."

"Perhaps we've spent too much time together." Her lips turned up slightly.

"Too much is not enough." Despite confusion swirling among my emotions and beliefs, my hand edged across the table and touched her arm. "I still love you, Essie."

We were quiet for a long time—circumnavigating the globe in our own thoughts. Were we destined to land safely in each other's world or project out of orbit, spiraling alone into space?

Everything was so raw and torn open now, any other wonderings deserved to be asked. "Did you know the other boy's family … Phil's?"

"Yes, not close friends, more like acquaintances even though the boys spent a lot of time together. After the funeral, I'd see his mother in the grocery store sometimes, but we'd pretend not to notice the other. I suppose it was too hard for either of us to go there." She paused, swiping at tears rolling down her cheeks. "Horrible really. That poor woman … she never knew what was the catalyst for her son's death."

I narrowed my eyes, trying to understand the full connection.

"Lou, even though the boys were in Phil's car," she grimaced. "Reece was the driver. He was the one speeding and lost control before they hit the tree."

My chair, though cushioned, suddenly felt hard. *Two young lives lost. Senseless. No … my action made it three. Four?* I shifted in my chair, realizing the guilt and pain would never go away when it came to my own son. *Could I, would I, have altered Michael's life course to spare him the horrors of war for the chance he would be with me now? Possibly … yes. Long ago, with nothing more than a shove, I'd changed the course of another's life … never giving thought to the consequences.*

Essie gazed out the window, seemingly lost in her thoughts. "Junior High. The boys were on the same baseball team, and then the older Reece got, the less I seemed to know of his life … his friends, what they were up to." She turned and looked at me. "But Phil ate dinner with us once in a while. Nice young man. Handsome too."

"And Ray?" I gestured toward his photograph propped on the credenza. "How was he after the accident?"

Clearly, I stepped into delicate territory. Essie slowly pushed herself from the table, her back to me. "He was devastated. Thought it was his fault, Reece leaving that night so upset." She turned toward me, and my heart split in two at the sorrow on her face. "For years, I tried to bring myself to tell my husband what I'd done." Her eyes opened wide. "Regardless of the reason the military rejected Reece, the same argument would have most likely happened … none of it made sense, it just …"

"Why couldn't you tell him, Essie?"

Wringing her hands, it was as if she pleaded with me to help sort through the deceit and pain. "Allie asked me the same thing … and I told her that her father would have hated me because we disagreed about the war. To me, it was senseless so many Americans had died and thousands more would follow. I wasn't one of those long-haired hippies carrying signs in the streets." She covered her heart with both hands. "It was more about fear … not wanting my son's name included in hushed conversations along with another boy we knew—Trey Neumann—he graduated from high school with my son … killed by sniper fire."

I bowed my head and thought about Betty. If I had encouraged her to share what was on her heart when Michael's number was called, she probably would have felt the same.

"But maybe I never told Ray because he loved me so much, and I was the only one, besides Allie, he had left. For weeks after the funeral, Ray hardly spoke." She walked over and held Ray's photograph. "But eventually, like Allie and I were his only source of oxygen, he breathed us in—more loving and attentive than he'd ever been."

I understood, remembering how, after Michael was buried, I'd burrow my head into Betty's chest as we lay in bed, listening to her breath and falling asleep to her heartbeat.

Essie turned and looked at me. Methodically, she reset the picture frame, smoothed the front of her blouse, and tugged at her sleeves. "So, Lou, now that we've revealed our tainted pasts, where does that leave us?"

My turn to pause and reflect. Her question was valid, but cutting—digging as though exposing a festering splinter—unseen by others for so many years, yet always present and painful.

I weighed my response. "Forgiven." The word sounded foreign yet peaceful as it passed from my lips.

Her shoulders lowered, and her frown relaxed before echoing my plea, "Forgiven."

Like sheep in need of a shepherd, we wandered around the room. She made several trips to the sink with too few dishes. I refolded the newspaper too many times. Finally, as two lost souls stumbling through a dark forest, we stepped into a clearing, found each other, and embraced—holding on for dear life and looking above to the light.

I felt compelled to do something else—a response that only recently had become part of my life. "Do you have a Bible in the house?"

"Yes." Her voice was wary. "On my nightstand. Why?"

As fast as a bona fide senior citizen can shuffle on high-pile carpet, I took off down the hall, then returned from her bedroom with a black leather book in hand. "You need to hear this." The couch facing the wide picture window was the perfect place to share the story. "Here, sit down with me."

"What are you up to?" She edged next to me.

"Bible reading has never been at the top of my list"—I flipped the pages—"but Hank convinced me I should try it. Spend less time on the computer now, but I'm learning to enjoy the stories. I slowed at Second Samuel, chapter eleven. "That King David ... I like that guy, but he messed up royally."

"That's a bad pun." Essie gave me a slight elbow.

"He lusted for the beautiful Bathsheba. He was enticed by something, and in his case, someone he believed he had to have. He went to a great length to get what he wanted."

"I'm not sure where you're going with this, but neither you nor I intended for those boys to—"

"Die? Like David had Bathsheba's husband killed in battle?"

She shook her head. "Poor Uriah. I'm sure he dearly loved his wife."

"Essie." I continued turning pages and stopped at Psalm fifty-one, verse four. "This might sound crazy, but as I was flipping through the Bible before we went to Mexico—the one Betty took with her to church—I came to the only section of Scripture she'd ever marked."

Essie's eyebrows arched as she leaned in.

"To her, it was disrespectful to write on God's Word." I shrugged. "I don't think it matters. Anyway, listen to what David said, 'Against you,

you only, have I sinned and done what is evil in your sight so you are right in your verdict and justified when you judge.'"

"Okay, so we're off the hook with each other, but not with God." She rubbed at her temples. "That's depressing."

"Without going further, I would have agreed. Bless her heart, Betty had underlined more, 'Surely I was sinful at birth, sinful from the time my mother conceived me. Yet you desired faithfulness even in the womb; you taught me wisdom in that secret place. Cleanse me with hyssop, and I will be clean; wash me, and I will be whiter than snow.'" My voice quivered. "Essie, do you know what that last part meant to me?" Her hand slipped into mine. "Those words set me free."

My forefinger rested on verse ten. "Read to the end with me, Essie."

"Of the whole Bible?" She winked.

Together, we read aloud, "Create in me a pure heart, O God, and renew a steadfast spirit within me. Do not cast me from your presence or take your Holy Spirit from me. Restore to me the joy of your salvation and grant me a willing spirit, to sustain me."

Our eyes locked as though a silent vow had been sealed.

"Eloquent, that King David. He found favor with God." I closed the Bible. "But for the first time in my life, I've allowed myself to come before the throne of God."

She nodded as though she understood. "Then we should kneel."

"Here?" I pointed to the floor.

"Why not?" Essie gracefully slid her bottom off the couch and balanced on her knees. I followed suit, but with much less finesse.

"For a long time, I've been trying to be holy—showing up each Sunday and taking up space in the pew." Her face reddened. "And I'm not too proud of it, Lou. Do you wonder if God was up to something … having our lives run parallel for years, then bringing us together?"

"I think so. No other way to explain it."

At first, I thought she'd lost her balance as she went onto her hands and knees, and then lay prostrate on the floor. But as she began praying, I did the same, adding my own prayer that I'd be able to stand again.

In the middle of thanks for grace and mercy, the door behind us slammed, followed by a scream. "Oh my God, what's happened?" Allie's high-pitched panic sent us rolling onto our sides. We exchanged surprised looks and then burst into laughter.

"What in the world are you two doing?" She stood over us, clutching a bag of groceries to her chest. "You scared me to death—thought I'd walked in on a double heart attack."

Essie laughed so hard a snort ensued, which in turn nearly had me wetting my pants.

Allie only rolled her eyes and plopped the bag on the counter.

"Good grief, can't an old couple have a bit of fun?" Essie pushed herself onto her knees and then upright. I took a little longer, grateful for the couch's sturdy support.

"Your mother and I were simply having a roll around in the hay. Right, honey?"

Essie's reply was a playful swat.

"Well, whatever you were doing, don't do it again." Groceries began to fill the kitchen counter. "Gave me the creeps."

"You, a romance writer?" I enjoyed poking fun at Allie. She was a good sport.

"I've never had characters do that in any of my books."

"You ought to let them try—might boost sales." An air drumroll followed. "But if you really want to know the truth, your mom and I were—"

"What are the groceries for?" Essie waylaid my thought and squeezed my arm.

Agreed. The sacred moment was between Essie, me, and God.

Chapter Thirty-Three

Essie ~ Letting Go

I know my daughter, and her armload of groceries sufficed as a modern-day peace offering. She had nothing to be sorry about, and I was relieved she'd come for a truce. After items were stowed away in the pantry and freezer, the intended necessities, utensils, and bowls took over the countertop. At least today, no mention was made of our last encounter. Instead, our emotional-wound bandages remained in place. More massaging, healing, and care would be needed after that big of a blow.

After small talk about the weather and if the Colorado Rockies were destined to have a good season, Allie zeroed in and dropped a bomb of her own.

"Peter's been offered a new job." She stirred the chicken-salad mixture a bit too vigorously. "He wanted to tell you about it himself, but he's catching an early flight to New York in the morning."

"New York?" I beamed at the thought of the fashion district where my friend, Stella, frequented before she'd retired and closed her boutique. "Did he get promoted to the buying position he's always wanted?"

"Sort of." She continued to stir, much too consumed with the contents of the bowl.

"Allie, why's he in New York?" *Would I ever shake mother's intuition that there was more to a story than being told?*

"Because we're moving there at the end of the summer." The spatula stalled. "For him to begin a new job with Bergdorf Goodman."

Lou settled into a kitchen chair, clearly not wanting to be a referee.

"Moving?" My voice raised a pitch. "Why didn't you tell me?"

"Mom, that's what I'm trying to do, and you're not making this any easier. You're the one who said Peter and I need a new adventure." She lifted a fork and stabbed a defenseless chunk of rotisserie meat. "Peter's been offered an amazing opportunity to not only manage but also buy for the entire shoe division—both women and men. He'd never land a job like this in Denver, plus he'll receive a substantial pay raise. He's been in the business a long time and deserves the recognition."

"How long have you known about this?" My stomach knotted.

"A few hours." She slid a piece of chicken off the fork and into her mouth. "I'm starving. How about you two?"

"That's not much time to make a decision like this." *Essie, get a hold of yourself.*

"It feels right, Mom. Peter's known about the opportunity for a few weeks but didn't want me to freak out if it fizzled. I know this seems spontaneous, but quite frankly, I'm feeling giddy at the thought of us living in the Big Apple."

"Well, it costs a fortune to live there, and what will Snowy do? You can't have a dog cooped up in a small apartment." My throat tightened at the thought of my daughter living far away.

"Snowy will be fine. She's tiny, doesn't need a lot of space. And Mom, you'll be all right." She glanced at Lou, who watched us like a spectator at a tennis match. "Because now you have him."

"True, but that's different." In my attempted defense, I sounded foolish. "I'm sorry, Lou. That's not what was meant."

"No offense taken. I'm a big boy. But think about it, honey, both of our daughters will be living in NYC, and we can visit."

His attempt to lighten the mood was appreciated, but hearing my daughter would no longer be fifteen or so minutes away was not my idea of good news. "Sweetie, I'm happy for Peter, and you're right, it sounds like a wonderful opportunity. You'll be closer to your publisher as well. Is that a factor in all of this?"

"Yes and no." Three plates were filled with chicken and fruit. "Technically, I can write from anywhere, but it would be easier to promote my books and meet with the editors and marketing team. The publishing industry gets more and more competitive."

"At least everyone still wants to fall in love." My fingers ran through her thick hair—the texture she'd inherited from me. "And yes, Lou and I have each other, but it won't be the same with you so far—"

"Mom, everything's going to be okay." Ice cubes plopped into her favorite iced tea with lemonade. "And the best part, Peter and I are excited about this change. Life had become so monotonous the last few years, and we agree a change of scenery will be good for us. To be honest, you two have reminded us there's plenty of life to live and lots of love ahead."

"Wow, sweetie. That's quite a testimony from someone who comes up with stories about falling in love."

Allie leaned against the counter. "*Stories*. That's the key word."

I conferred with Lou's blank look. "What do you mean?"

"I dream them up. The places might be real, or at least could be. But I make up the people, some to love, others to hate. I throw a whole bunch of problems at them." She folded her arms. "Some work out, others don't."

Lou gave an easy nod. "Sounds like life."

"So true." Allie winced. "And I'll admit, somewhere along the journey of having my protagonists live happily ever after, I bought into the fantasy that I deserved even better."

"And what's better than happily ever after?" I asked.

No one spoke. In fact, we looked at one another like dumbfounded contestants on *Family Feud*.

Finally, Allie spoke. Her voice was soft yet assured. "The only thing better than happily ever after is … living the truth … whatever that has to be."

We squeezed each other's hands and then settled around the table—a triad of love and commitment—able to withstand the distance to come.

Blinking back tears, I raised my glass. "Cheers."

"Cheers," my daughter echoed.

"*Cin cin*," the handsome Italian chimed in.

Chapter Thirty-Four

Lou ~ Popping Balloons

It was the right thing to call Jennifer, even though I was determined not to let her change my mind. Pushing the speed-dial button to her cell number, I braced myself for a lecture.

"Hello." Her girly voice lifted like wispy clouds on a summer's day.

I still love the sound of her voice.

"Hey, honey."

"Something wrong? It's not Sunday."

"Not at all. Just have something to talk with you about." I cleared my throat. "Is this a good time?"

"Actually, a call should be coming in any time now from the twins and Carl. We're having an important conference call."

"Do you own a family enterprise of which I'm unaware? You seem to have a lot of these very important *meetings*."

"Dad, it's pretty hard for the four of us to have a discussion when we're scattered all over the country."

"Where's Carl?"

"At home."

"Then, where are you?"

"In Dallas." Her voice dropped. "For a while. I'm staying with a girlfriend. She's a photographer as well. Said I could stay in the guest room until I figure things out."

The daddy in me lifted a protective guard as my chest puffed out, and I paced the family room. "And what exactly does that mean?"

"Don't get mad ... but it means I need some time away ... from my marriage."

Mad? Was that the response she assumed from me, and why she hadn't talked with me first before allowing this to happen?

"Jen, I'm saddened to hear this, but I'm not mad ... unless one of you've had—"

"Daddy!"

I'd hit a tender nerve. "I'm sorry, but that happens all the time. I don't live in a bubble." My next question came with caution. "Is something going on with Carl?"

"I don't think so, I mean it's both of us." Her sigh traveled across our distance. "We've decided taking a little break might be good for us. The kids agree."

"And why would they want that?" Fortunately, my daughter couldn't see my head shaking in disapproval. "They're not even home any longer to be involved on a daily basis."

"True, but lots of their friends' parents have done the same. Apparently, this is common for empty nesters."

"Jen, I don't understand. If there hasn't been an affair, and he's kind to you ... he is kind to you, right?"

"He is, and I'm civil to him as well."

"Being civil is hardly loving," I retorted, and her silence gave me reason to wait.

"That's the problem." A few sniffles followed.

"Honey, you've lost me. What's exactly going on? I thought you really love him. Especially the way you've taken care of Carl ever since—"

"Dad, do you remember the movie that always made us cry, the one about the little boy who loved his red balloon?"

Memory has a way of anchoring one to the past, and the short French film appropriately titled *The Red Balloon*, came floating back to mind as if Jennifer and I were cuddled on the sofa, tears streaming down our cheeks.

"I'll never forget." My words came delicately, like the boy who had held his deflated, yet beloved balloon at the climax of the film.

"Carl and I seem to be out of each other's reach." Her voice shook, balancing conviction and crying. "And when we think we've worked things out, we can't seem to hold on to each other."

Images from the poignant film filled my mind. A sad and lonely boy, befriended by a big red balloon that followed him, in stark comparison, along the black and white avenues and alleys of Paris. A beautiful yet brief friendship—happy, content, and safe—until a band of ruffians threw rocks at the balloon. I remember feeling a bit foolish, crying along with my daughter as the balloon deflated, dying in the arms of the boy who loved it so much.

"And what doesn't make sense about all of this, I think I'm drifting away from him … like my heart will be safer if I'm farther away."

The film's ending scene was as clear as if I were watching it again—balloons, scores of them, unleashing from balloon vendors and pulling free from the hands of children in parks—brightly colored balloons from all over Paris, gathering around the boy and lifting him high above the magnificent city and far away from the cruel world below.

"Daddy, I could never say this to Carl, but I'm really afraid of him dying … someday much sooner than he should. Considering his health issues, he's an incredibly strong man. He goes to the office every day, works long hours, provides for the kids and me. But that's part of the problem. He doesn't stop working. This meeting, that conference, another dinner with clients, early breakfast meeting with the creative team. I know it sounds cliché, but I wonder if he loves his career more than he loves me."

A deep exhale followed. "I know what you're thinking, Daddy. I'm a horrible person and why in the world don't I want to support and help my husband. Why wouldn't I sacrifice my own life, care for my spouse when things get worse, just like you did for Mom?"

Like mother, like daughter. As with Betty, Jennifer could talk a mile a minute when she was upset. But somewhere along the marathon of life, Jennifer outpaced even her mother's dialogues when it came to intense emotions. I settled into my recliner, prepared for the onslaught. Better to listen first and try to make sense of my daughter's state of affairs.

A nose-blowing on the other end of the line allowed a reprieve before she continued. "I'm staying with my friend, Susie. She and I met at the Photographers' Guild, but she got divorced last month and decided going back to her home state is the best option. Said she preferred being around the Texas drawl than the *Noo Yawker's* accent. I'm keeping her company while she gets over being alone. I tell you, the divorce thing is hard, but I can't imagine being a widow … especially at my age. Maybe if Carl and I were old it would be easier."

"It's not." My response slipped out—the subconscious truth—too powerful to simply listen any longer. I swallowed hard.

"Daddy, I'm sorry." A long sigh followed. "If I'm completely honest … I'm scared. It was so hard when Mom was really sick … I don't know if I'm strong enough to deal with it again … I don't know what I'll do when he—"

"And running away is the answer?" My voice was flat.

"No." Another long pause. "Just a break. To figure things out."

"Jen?"

"Ya, Daddy?"

"Don't give up on him. Don't toss out your marriage because all the parts aren't working just right."

Odd to think how easily a thing like love is discarded. Like a pair of once stylish and expensive shoes, despite the polishing and prime placement on the closet shoe rack, the miles of walking eventually break them in, then down. And one day, there's a hole in the sole, and the shoes end up in the trash bin. Another pair takes up residency—has its glory days—until it too is forgotten, set aside, no longer shiny and new.

"Sweetheart, do you and Carl love each other?" The question was simple, but with age comes wisdom.

Her voice was barely audible, but her reply was clear. "We do."

"Then maybe that's reason enough to persevere." Right then, the distance between us was too far. My daughter needed my embrace as much as I needed hers.

"Thanks for talking, Daddy. I'll be in touch soon and let you know what's happening."

"Jennifer, I think—"

"Daddy, I promise I'll call soon."

"Bye, hon." My voice caught. "I love you."

"Love you, too … oh, I didn't even ask why you were calling."

"We can talk another time." Whether young or grown, your child's needs always take precedence, and that's okay.

"No, really. Fill me in."

I hesitated, not sure I wanted to pop another balloon. "Well, since we're on the subject … Essie and I are getting married." There, the air was out.

"I'm not surprised." Her voice was matter of fact. "Actually, I was wondering when you'd spill the beans. You've been scared to tell me, haven't you?"

A breath of fresh air seemed to fill the room. "A little."

"Have you set a date?"

"Sometime this summer, sooner than later."

"That's like now. Weddings take planning."

"Jen, it's not like we're young and have tons of people to invite." The thought was morbid, but I had to laugh. "We've outlived many so … more cake for us."

"Really?" Her sass had returned, and for that I was glad.

"Really." Now the serious part returned to my mind. "But first, I need to ask her properly —a gentleman's proposal for a beautiful bride-to-be."

I glanced at two framed photos on my side table. Not much of a photographer, I'd snapped an off-centered, cockeyed picture of Essie as she sat in a beach chair sipping a margarita. Big sunglasses, windblown hair, and a sun-kissed face. She was beautiful.

The other picture was taken by the resort photographer who had suckered us into having our photo taken with his pet iguana. The expensive picture, worth every penny, captured the three of us— wrinkled, scaly, and prehistoric.

"Sounds like we both have some reporting to do. Good luck with that, Daddy. I'm sure you'll sweep her off her feet."

"Goodbye, Jen." As the call ended, my heart felt as though a heartstring had snapped.

Chapter Thirty-Five

Essie ~ A Gift from the Sea

Preparations for Allie and Peter's move to New York were nearly complete. Boxes packed, the house under contract, and my full allotment of tears shed.

Cooking classes with Lou kept me busy on Tuesday and Thursday afternoons. Saturday evenings were reserved for trying the recipes and techniques at one of our homes.

"Let's go out to dinner tonight instead." Lou had arrived twenty minutes early with a particularly stunning bouquet of red roses.

"What's the occasion?" The heady scent wafted to my nose as I carried them to the kitchen. "Doesn't braised chicken *all'arrabbiata* sound good?"

"What the instructor failed to mention is *all'arrabbiata* means "in angry style." Lou scrunched his nose and eyes, pretending a mean look.

"And she failed to realize you are a full-blooded Italian."

He spread his arms wide and sang in his best, off-key imitation of Luciano Pavarotti, "*Dilegua, oh notte! Tramontate, stelle! Tramontate, stelle! All'alba vincerò! Vincerà! Vincerò!*" Lou could pull energy from his pocket, and tonight he was on.

"How do you still remember all that Italian? You haven't spoken it since you were a child, have you?"

"Not really. I've kept the phrases that are important to the heart. And I listen to a lot of the Three Tenors—they are so good." He thumped his hand over his heart.

"Lou Rizzo, there is still a lot that is mysterious about you. And I have no idea what you sang."

"In short, it means for the night to depart, and in the morning, there will be triumph." He bowed, completing his short-lived performance. "But tonight is still young, and we need to celebrate—no room for angry chicken."

"Anything in particular we're celebrating?" He kissed my cheek.

"Only us, *il mia amore*."

* * * * *

An earlier light rain had turned into steady drizzle as we ducked into the Fresh Fish Company. The hostess seated us at a secluded table, far from the noise near the bar.

"I haven't been here in years. Ray and I came here on our birthdays. Did you know they give your age as the percentage off?"

"At our age, we'll be eating for pennies." Lou's eyes widened. "Maybe we should leave and come back next month when you turn eighty-one. Or better yet, let's hold out for mine. Eighty-three percent off is a bargain."

"No, I'm looking forward to eating here, especially the famous sourdough bread." My mouth watered at the thought. "I'm glad we can share openly about our spouses. They were both special people who brought a lot of happiness to our lives."

"Yes." A smile of contentment settled on his face. "We were fortunate to have long and loving marriages. That doesn't happen much these days."

He proceeded to fill me in about Jennifer and Carl. The topic made him edgy, especially since his daughter hadn't called to give an update.

"We'll have to say some extra prayers for them." My eyes lowered as a gentle reminder of my hypocrisy tapped me on the shoulder. "It's different now."

"What do you mean?"

"Prayer." The word was reverent as it left my lips.

"For me as well. Amazing to realize I'm actually speaking with God."

After the waitress poured our Chardonnays, detailed the chef's specials, and then excused herself to give us time to consider the menu, we lifted our glasses and toasted the night.

"Good idea to go out." I sipped my wine. "Doing dishes is overrated."

Then, like a magician, Lou's hand hovered over the white tablecloth. He raised his hand, and sitting between us was a beautiful seashell—bleached yet unbroken—perfectly created and whole.

"Go ahead. Pick it up." His eyes lit.

I ran my fingertip over the smooth shell, awed by the intricate, delicate design. "Remember all the seashells we saw on vacation? The ocean washed them to shore as if it were giving us gifts."

"Turn it over, Essie." His voice was gentle but eager.

I rolled the shell over, and like an escaped treasure from a long-forgotten, sunken chest, a beautiful diamond ring sparkled at me. "Oh, Lou …"

"Don't you like it?" His brow creased. "We can get another one if you don't."

"It's absolutely perfect." I slipped it on my left ring finger that for so many years wore a ring from another love.

He took my hands in his and spoke the words I'd never imagined to hear again. "Essie, will you marry me?"

"I would love to marry you, Joseph Marino …" *Always good to keep a man on his toes.* My smile came naturally. "I'd be honored to be your wife, Lou Rizzo."

"We'll keep each other young and laughing, won't we?"

"Laughing, yes. Young? I'll do my best."

"Fair enough." He kissed the top of my hands.

"Where did you get such a beautiful shell?" I lifted the iridescent shell toward the flickering candle in the small votive.

"Mexico. Most of the shells were broken, but I found this one right before we left on the shuttle. Meant to be—the perfect one." He leaned forward and inspected the shimmering colors along with me. "Good thing customs didn't frisk me. They would have confiscated it as contraband."

"Taking shells is illegal?"

"I'm not sure, but if so"—a mischievous grin spread across his face—"then it's our little secret."

The waitress must have been taking in bits and pieces of our conversation. When she approached our table, she beamed as though we were celebrities, and, admittedly, I felt special.

"Looks like congratulations are in order." She dabbed at her eyes with the wine cloth. "Sorry, I usually don't cry at work, but the two of you are the cutest things I've ever seen."

I understood her compliment, but Lou cocked his head as if the waitress had likened us to a pair of stuffed animals at a carnival booth.

She lifted the wine bottle and refilled our glasses. "My parents had just celebrated their fiftieth anniversary when my dad passed. I wish my mom could find someone as wonderful as you." Her hand touched Lou's shoulder.

My heart warmed as my husband-to-be beamed. "He is wonderful, isn't he?"

"Never too late." He nodded at me. "Right, doll?"

The meal and each other's company couldn't have been better. Our cooking classes had turned us into junior sleuths. As we tasted the assortment of fish and sides, we discussed which ingredients and techniques the chef might have used to work his wonders.

"Seasoning's the trick." Lou ran his tongue over his lips. "Just the right mixture."

Chapter Thirty-Six

When Essie first mentioned the idea of us hosting an intimate dinner party in place of a reception, the traditional side of me balked. But as the plans came together for an August fourth wedding—allowing us a little over a month to invite our family and close friends—it felt right.

Together, with the help of our quirky cooking instructor, appropriately named Olive Rosemary Marie (although I suspected it was a stage name), we set the menu. Fortunately, my Scottish-Welsh bride-to-be loved Italian food as much as she loved me, so agreeing on what to serve came easily. The only element that gave me pause was her insistence that the dessert be oatmeal-chocolate-chip cookies—hardly Italian, but a family recipe of hers that, I had to admit, was beyond good.

"Another thing I love about you, Lou. You go with the flow." She sealed the last envelope from the list of invitees and pressed on a stamp. "I'm glad we invited Arlene and that nice man she's been dating. If she hadn't given you a kick in the pants to ask me out, we might both be with someone else."

Lou made a pretend sad face, but we both knew we'd most likely be alone had not fate or, truthfully, God opened the doors.

I hope Hank and Libby will be back in town. Those two have been traveling like there's no tomorrow."

"Hank told me they'd cut the trip to Santa Fe short if they had to." With my tennis shoe propped on the edge of the chair, I bent slightly to tighten the lace. "Speaking of no tomorrow, what do you think about us doing something big for a honeymoon?"

"We'll, we've already been to Mexico, and that could serve as the getaway."

"Naw." I swiped my hand in the air. "That's too practical, and we need to treat ourselves. I have plenty of money in the bank, and so do you."

"Since when have you been looking?" She pursed her lips. "If you think you're marrying a rich girl, you're wrong."

"And if you're thinking the same, then we've both been fooled." With my hands on her shoulders, I rubbed tight muscles. "But the best part is, even though we've agreed to keep things simple and our assets apart, neither one of us is taking any of it to the grave, so we might as well enjoy what we have now."

She rolled her shoulders and tilted her head. "Agreed, and that brings up one unanswered question we've both been avoiding."

"I know. Where are we going to live?"

Understandably, neither of us wanted to sell our home. Both houses were roomy, maintained well, and, at least to our own standards, decorated stylishly. Where it was difficult to budge, though, was that each of our homes over the many years we'd lived in them had become … comfortable. Like an old pair of favorite garden gloves, our homes were familiar. And despite the worn patches and small rips and tears, they were what we'd come to know.

She pushed away from the table. "How about we take a walk? I haven't been exercising like I should." She patted her tummy. "Plus, I need to trim down so I can fit in my wedding gown."

The expression on my face must have surprised her as much as her comment did me.

"I'm only kidding. This old gal won't be gliding down the aisle like I just jumped off a wedding cake." She turned in a circle. "But my dress will be lovely, don't you worry."

"You could wear a burlap sack, and I'd be happy. Speaking of which, I'd better see how my uniform fits. Haven't had it on since last year's Tenth Mountain reunion."

"Are you really going to wear it?" She wrapped her arms around my waist. "It's hard to resist a man in uniform."

"For you, I'll make it fit."

"Colonel Lou Rizzo, you'll be my Prince Charming."

Essie had a way of making me feel ten times lighter. "That's Retired

Colonel Lou Rizzo."

"Even better." She perched on her tiptoes and kissed me. "More time for us."

* * * * *

A short jaunt around the neighborhood turned out to be lucky. A few blocks to the south, a small ranch-style home, with flowers in front and a large shady tree, was on the market.

"For Sale … cozy and comfortable." I read the sales pitch aloud. "Sounds like the place for us."

Essie pulled her phone from her jacket pocket and snapped a photo, something I always seemed to forget those cell phones could do. "Let's peek in the front window."

"They may be home. Let's not go snooping around." I stood on the sidewalk as she followed the curving path leading to the front door.

"They're hardly going to call the police and have two old Peeping Toms arrested." She pushed the doorbell. "Let's see if anyone's home."

No telling what this woman of mine will do next.

A young man answered the door, joined shortly by a woman. A toddler with tangled blond hair clung tightly to her mother's leg.

"Can we help you? We saw you looking at the sign." The man stepped onto the porch.

I caught up to Essie and answered, "Sorry to bother you—"

"Looks like someone just woke up from a nap." Essie smiled at the little girl.

"Or needs one," the mother replied, running her hands over her protruding belly. "What I'd give for a long rest myself."

"I remember those days, sleep as precious as gold." Essie bent toward the tiny child and waved a slight wave. "I bet you'll fall fast asleep after a good story, right?"

The girl squirmed and pursed her cherub lips into a smile.

"She's a cutie." I extended my hand. "I'm Lou, and this is my fiancée, Essie. She lives around the corner. We were out walking and noticed your beautiful home is for sale."

I think I'd lost them back at *fiancée* because both of their mouths were slightly open.

"You're getting married? Congratulations."

"That's amazing," the woman added. "I mean … that's wonderful. When's the big day?"

"August fourth," I said. "We're trying to get our living situation in order."

"You don't already have a house?" She shifted the toddler to the other leg. "I mean, you're not living together."

Essie and I exchanged glances, and had it not been rude, we both would have laughed. "No, we're doing it the old-fashioned way—keeping separate residences until legally husband and wife."

"That's cool," the man said, nodding at the woman. "Isn't it, babe?"

"Yeah, my mom and dad did that. Weren't too happy about us having kids first, but we've been talking about marriage, haven't we?"

"Yep." The man smiled boyishly and pushed his hands into his pockets. "Anyway, I'm Sean and this is Katie. The little one is Dory."

"After Dory the fish, you know, the funny little fish in the movie *Finding Nemo*."

Like creatures from another planet, Essie and I could only shrug and smile.

"Anyway, it's a great movie—you should rent it sometime." Little Dory had clearly had enough of the small talk and tugged at her mother's shorts.

"We won't keep you any longer, but how about if we take one of the fliers and contact the agent?"

"Absolutely." Sean trotted down the walk and pulled a piece of paper from the box attached to the sign. "I'm super good with handyman work and have the place all fixed up." He turned his palms upward and pointed to calluses. "See, the marks of a hardworking man."

"Good for you, Sean." I shook his hand. "Nothing wrong with hard work to keep a good man honest and taking care of his family."

✷ ✷ ✷ ✷ ✷

A few weeks later, Essie and I became the proud owners of the little ranch house with flowers and a shady tree in front. Sean, Katie, and little Dory ended up moving only a few blocks away into a larger house. After Lou and I settled into our new house, we promised to have them over for supper and lend a hand with Dory when the new baby arrived—kneading the generations together and adding more flavor to one another's lives.

Chapter Thirty-Seven

Essie ~ Until Death Do Us Part

Jennifer, Carl, and the kids arrived at the church together—a good sign since the topic of a separation hadn't been brought up lately, and Lou didn't want to ask. Now that the twins were home for the summer, perhaps time spent as a family had helped—vacations to Long Island beaches and drives upper state surely had slowed the pace of their hectic lives.

"You are stunning." Jennifer's soft voice slipped in the half-open doorway leading into the dressing room to the side of the sanctuary.

"Come in, dear." With my face only inches from the full-length mirror, I touched up my makeup and ran a comb through my hair. "I'm used to my magnifying mirror. Can hardly see a thing." I looked at the stylish woman in the reflection behind me, her hair swept up with curled tendrils framing defined cheekbones. "Jennifer, you look wonderful."

"Here, you have a little smudge of mascara," she said, gently wiping my eyelid. "And the pink lipstick is the perfect color with the lavender dress. Essie, before the ceremony, I wanted to say"—she paused and walked across the small room—"you inspire me."

She had sparked my curiosity, but I didn't speak.

"I don't know you well, and I hope we have plenty of opportunities to change that, but there's a lot to learn from a woman like you."

"How so?"

She gently touched my small bouquet, a cluster of white and pink roses, intertwined with sprigs of soothing lavender, waiting on the counter. "Because you are brave enough to love again."

I returned to my reflection and smiled at the woman in the mirror. Long gone was my long brown hair and taut smooth skin. Areas sagged and slightly bulged where gravity once had no place. *It is well with my soul.* The phrase from an old hymn washed over, bathing me like the fountain of youth. Jennifer watched me, her silhouette behind mine, just as she was in a time of life that had once been part of mine.

"Brave? I don't know … but blessed, I'm sure."

She handed me the bouquet, chosen by Lou, and gifted to me this morning. "I'm happy for you and Daddy." We hugged—a woman-to-woman embrace that confirmed we shared similar hopes and dreams.

"We'd better get you out there. You know my father and his military time."

* * * * *

Blow me over with a breath of air. When I saw my husband-to-be in his dress blues uniform, I swooned like a schoolgirl … again. Lou Rizzo, the mysterious heartthrob of Golden High School, and I were about to be married.

The number of guests was small, but at that moment, with Allie standing next to me, and Hank as Lou's best man, it was as if we were among the multitudes—a perfect world in a perfect place.

Pastor Jeff stood in front of us, the Bible open in his hands. And when the vows were read and repeated, the words played like a melody of a favorite love song in my mind.

"I, Lou, take you, Essie, for my lawful wife, to have and to hold, from this day forward, for better, for worse, for richer, for poorer, in sickness and health, until death do us part."

"I, Essie, take you, Lou, for my lawful husband, to have and to hold, from this day forward, for better, for worse, for richer, for poorer, in sickness and health, until death do us part."

The tender way he held my hand made me feel like a queen. Still, after all the years, and having shared similar words before, my legs trembled beneath my floor-length skirt—not with fear, but with excitement about our future. Hopefully, many more years of good health lay ahead. Sickness would come, eventually bringing its bedfellow, death. But for now, Lou and I were fully alive, and all was well with our souls.

* * * * *

"Oh, Ginny." I ran my thumb under her right eye. "You were crying, weren't you?"

"Such a beautiful ceremony, Ess. I'm so happy for you." Her typical bear hug enveloped me, and I laughed. "Phyllis and I miss spending time with you now that you have that handsome man in your life. Don't we, Phil?"

"Of course, we do, but we understand." Phyllis gave me a peck on the cheek, her burgundy lipstick most likely leaving a mark.

"When I'm back from the honeymoon, how about we have a girls' night out?"

"Deal. Maybe we can tear up the town. Haven't done that in years." Ginny laughed so hard she let out a snort-sniffle.

I gently swatted my friend. "Let's just not get arrested."

"Have you ever told Lou about the time the three of us got kicked out of the movie theater for talking too much?" Phyllis eyed me as though the crime of the century had been committed.

"No," I whispered. "He doesn't have to know *everything*, does he?"

"Good idea. Our secret." Ginny pinched my arm. "A little mystery keeps us alluring."

Phyllis raised her brows. "And that's why Ginny reads all those romance mysteries."

"You ought to try them, Phil." Ginny smirked. "I've met several very intriguing men."

Chapter Thirty-Eight

Essie ~ Salt and Pepper

While Lou and I swarmed around the kitchen like bees in a hive, Peter and Allie put finishing touches on the table. The other ten relaxed on the patio, enjoying the waning sun and antipasto platters of olives and bruschetta before dinnertime.

Admittedly, both of us were spent from the ceremony earlier in the day and now cooking for our reception. Ordering in or reserving the backroom at Viva Dolce would have been easier, but the aromas rising from the stovetop and oven gave us a second wind. Within minutes, we'd all be in gastronomic heaven.

The day before, Allie and Peter had hauled up the dining room table leaves from the basement, extending my mother's antique table to its restored glory days when families lived close and gathered often for special meals.

Unearthed from boxes on storage shelves, crystal and china were aligned in perfect rows. Sterling silver, unveiled from soft blue cloth that kept tarnish at bay, shined on either side of the dinner and salad plates. Peter, always with a stylish flair, had sculpted the linen napkins in such a way that one would have imagined Michelangelo himself was invited to join the affair. Nameplates, written in calligraphy, had been added by Allie—thoughtfully placed to mix up our tossed salad of sorts.

Lou was intent on adding the finishing touch—a special floral arrangement gifted by his "personal" florist at City Mart. A cascading bouquet of pink and white lilies, cobalt blue delphiniums, and lush greenery cradled spectacular sunflowers—each yellow burst spread open as if wishing a future of warmth and good fortune.

"Dinner is served," Lou announced from the open, sliding glass door.

Carl, Jennifer, Matt, and Liz entered first, followed by Ginny and Phyllis, Arlene and boyfriend Rich, then Hank and Libby.

"Everyone, find your place." Allie gestured to the table as Peter poured glasses of wine.

"Before you all sit, and Essie and I serve the salad, let's pray."

We stood around the table, hands joined and heads bowed as Lou offered the prayer. "Lord, we gather as a group of family and friends who have tremendous love for one another. And we give thanks for the mercy and grace You continue to shower on us. I give special thanks that Essie's now my wife." He squeezed my hand. "And may You bless this food. Amen."

"Amen," was the unifying encore, followed by Ginny's remark, "And bless the cooks."

Warm, crusty bread was passed around as Lou and I arranged the goat cheese and herb-stuffed radicchio leaves on plates.

"You've really stepped it up from the usual at Viva Dolce, hey, Lou?" Hank poked at the greenery, seemingly a bit mystified how to wrangle the salad.

"Wait 'til the main course." Lou tightened his red, green, and white striped apron scrawled with the words, *Buon appetito!*"

"I'm afraid you'll never want to go back to our old favorite." Although Hank joked, there was some truth that he and Lou's routine had missed a few beats since Libby and I cut into their dance.

"Not a chance, buddy. In fact, I miss seeing spaghetti hang from your mouth."

* * * * *

After *Zuppa di Vongole*, *Fettuccine con Carciofi*, and Spinach Risotto filled our bellies, the twelve of us leaned back in unison and moaned.

"Love artichokes." Carl smiled across the table at his wife. "Jen's made them this summer a couple of times, haven't you, hon?"

I made a mental note as she returned a genuine smile to Carl. Perhaps they had ridden the wave of marital challenge to a peaceful cove.

"I steam them whole until the leaves pull off easily. Then we dip them in a garlic, lemon, and butter sauce. The kids gobble them up."

Lou winked at me. I knew he'd talked with Jennifer several times since her return from what she preferred to call her *retreat* to Dallas. He was hopeful from his conversations with her, and even with Carl late into the evenings, that his daughter and son-in-law would be steadfast in their commitment to each other and more sensitive to one another's needs.

"I've never tasted clams so good." Arlene eyed her empty bowl. "And to think those little rascals come from a shell."

"Plenty of good stuff comes from the sea." I held my wedding-ring-adorned hand to the group. "And a whole lot more." Even though Lou and I sat at opposite ends of the table, we may as well have been back on the beach, side by side, looking outward, but together in the same direction.

"Before we put ourselves completely over the edge with Essie's famous oatmeal- chocolate-chip cookies, let's toast." Lou lifted his glass. "Here's to this glorious day, nestled between fond memories of the past and hope for the future." He angled toward me and continued, "And to my beautiful wife, Essie, my constant, faithful companion …" He set his wine glass on the tablecloth, and in its place, held up a pair of salt and pepper shakers. "She is my salt and I, her pepper."

The others oohed and aahed at the eloquent toast. I tilted my glass toward the man who, if I was honest, most likely won my heart when he nicknamed me "Salt." Nearly a year ago. So much had changed.

"And to my handsome husband, Lou, who God gave to me as a reminder that there is a second chance at love." I looked around the table, taking in the faces of those most special in my life.

When Arlene nodded with me, my heart warmed for the woman who not only helped Lou maintain a tight ship but also helped keep his boat upright when the seas had been stormy.

Going forward, Lou and I hoped the new man in her life would continue to prove worthy. Rich had already survived a talk or two with the tough as nails, retired colonel.

Only two amongst the intimate gathering, Allie and Lou, knew my most raw and flawed self. The others would never know my secret—carried out to sea and buried deep within the ever-churning sand. As with Lou's past, his too was wiped clean—white as snow.

Lou's eyes locked with mine as if together we took a momentary stroll into our pasts, then turned, and waltzed into the future. "A second chance to love and be loved." He spoke softly, and I knew his words tonight were reserved for me.

Our trance was broken with Ginny clanging her wine glass with a fork.

Phyllis chimed in. "You know what that means, you two love birds.

Silly to be embarrassed at my age, but I felt my face redden as Lou stood and made his way to my end of the table.

"Well, hello, Salt." He puckered his lips.

I wrapped my hands around his neck and pulled him closer. "Well, hello to you, Pepper."

Cheers and whistles from the tiny crowd interrupted our private moment, and my husband, in his witty way, turned our backs to them and kissed me again.

There was a catcall from the audience. Then someone jested, "How about some dessert? We're starving here."

"Oh, Hank, you're such a hoot," Libby's bubbly voice called him out.

"Don't worry, Mom," Allie added, "you two keep kissing. Peter and I will serve dessert."

Chapter Thirty-Nine

Essie ~ Repainting the Past

Thank heaven for speakerphones. As we busied our hands packing, Allie and I chitchatted as mother and daughters do. Tomorrow, she left for New York, and the following day, I headed west.

"Got a new swimsuit at Kohl's," I said. "A pretty Hawaiian print."

"Good for you, Mom. You'll be the best-looking lady on the beach."

"Well, maybe the best in the advanced age category." I folded an aqua cover-up and placed it in the suitcase. "I'm excited to visit Kauai. It's called the Garden Isle …eternally in bloom with red hibiscus, purple and yellow orchids. One variety is called Show Stoppers, red ginger I think."

"You should paint while you're there."

"You know, that's been on my mind." I glanced at the speckles of dried paint on my fingertips—a reminder that I was up to my old tricks.

"But … everything's okay, right?" Allie prodded. "You know how you turn to painting when—"

"Everything's fine, sweetie. My life is better than good." I glanced at the nearly finished painting leaning against the wall in my study. I'd worked on it for several days since the wedding, between sorting items that would be moved to our new house next month.

"Remind me what time your flight is tomorrow," I said.

"Not until five. The shoe department team is throwing a lunchtime going away party for Peter."

"They're going to miss him."

"He's been good to all of them."

"He's a good man, Allie."

"You're right, Mom. He is."

The sound of suitcases being zipped filled the gap in our conversation.

"Then the timing is perfect. How about if I stop by in the morning? I have a gift for you."

"That's thoughtful, Mom, but I hope it will fit in my carry-on. The moving company picks up everything on Wednesday, and I'm already worried about what's going to fit in our apartment. You wouldn't believe what we're paying for a tiny place in Manhattan."

"I told you so." My words were melodic, and I smiled. *A mother always knows.*

"I know, I know."

* * * * *

Lou tried to wait up for me, but as artists-at-work do, strokes were added, values changed, and shading manipulated to make the painting just right. I'd found the Polaroid used as a reference to paint the family portrait in an overstuffed manila envelope in my old art class files.

I'd nearly missed the small picture until a funny intuition nudged me to reopen the envelope and search again. When I saw the image of my precious family, I cupped the small, glossy paper in both hands—like a delicate robin's egg that had fallen from its nest.

A long-forgotten childhood memory had flitted around my mind. Terse reminders from well-meaning, but know-it-all adults resounded from the past. *No use, little Essie. Even if you put the egg back in the nest, the mother will abandon it.*

I'd ignored the neighbors' facts and climbed high in the apple tree, the small blue egg wrapped in a kerchief I'd taken from my father's dresser drawer and gently wrapped around the egg before tucking it in the front pocket of my pinafore. My dress snagged and a button tore loose. But I didn't care. And when, in two weeks' time, young birds stretched their wings and flew from the high branches of the tree, my heart soared with them. I'd done the right thing. I knew it was time to do the right thing again.

I stood back and surveyed the completed painting—a precious family of four. Gently, I touched Ray's face—imagining running fingers through dark, wavy hair and pausing at lips that knew mine well.

"I miss you, Ray, but I'm okay now. That's what you would have wanted," I whispered into the night. "And, Allie, my angel child. You've grown into a beautiful woman—always my little girl, but forever my best friend."

My hand traveled to Reece, and as if going back in time, I wanted to immerse myself into the painting, wrap my arms around his slender shoulders and boyish body, pull him close—never let him go. Without repose, I slumped to my knees and sobbed—tears of remorse for all that should have been. For Reece, for Allie and Ray, and for me. Even though my life, in so many ways, had been blessed and continued to be, losing my child would forever leave an indelible wound.

* * * * *

The next morning when I pulled into Allie's driveway, I remained in the car as I second-guessed my decision to gift her the family portrait. When I'd come clean with her about Reece's death, her world was rocked. And, even though Allie had later insisted she'd forgiven me, I still wondered if my confession left a black hole between us—an unexplainable, mysterious void we'd continue to tiptoe around.

But when she approached my car and opened the passenger door, the decision was made.

"Mom, why haven't you come in? I saw you sitting out here and—" She stopped mid-sentence and stared at the painting propped along the backseat. "What's that? I mean, I know what it is, but—"

"For you." I unbuckled my seatbelt and shimmied out of the car.

She'd opened the back door, slid the painting out, and now held it up with both hands.

The morning sun bathed it in light, and although I noticed imperfections in my brushwork, Allie was riveted, her eyes locked with her brother's eyes.

I stood silently—an observer between the reunion of a brother and sister. Tears trickled down Allie's cheeks, and if the painted eyes of Reece could have cried, they would have done the same.

I should have known better. I shouldn't have caught her off guard like this. "Honey, I didn't mean to upset—"

"No, Mom." She lowered the painting, resting the frame against her legs. "It means more than anything in the world," she sniffed between words. "Reece is back … and so are you."

Like an endless slow dance, Allie and I clung to one another on the driveway and swayed.

Eventually, we uncurled our embrace and looked at one another.

"Do you remember when I asked you why you and Dad never

moved after Reece died?"

I folded my arms, not sure I wanted to revisit the day we'd talked, or more accurately, I'd pummeled her past.

"You never answered me, but I think I understand why you never moved." She looked down at the painting. "Lots of beautiful memories in that house—plenty of love and laughter—it wasn't all bad."

I looked down and surveyed the people in the painting—those whom I had laughed and cried with, those who knew me at my best and worst—the people I had loved the most.

"Allie, life and death are strange. One day, although different in an unbelievably wonderful way, you and I, Peter and Lou, too, we'll be with Reece and your dad. With the Lord's grace, the time we didn't have together here will be made up over and over."

"I want to believe that too, Mom." Her eyes narrowed as if to allow only what she could bear. "And the babies Peter and I never knew, they'll be there as well."

My hands went to the sides of my daughter's face. "Yes, those precious babies too."

If there was a void between us, it had disappeared. Our shared understanding and compassion for each other over past hurts, disappointments, trials, and even regrets had thrown us a lifeline. We'd been reunited.

＊ ＊ ＊ ＊ ＊

Allie called later to let me know she and Peter would take a taxi to the airport instead of having us drive.

"Peter probably thinks an old driver like me would make them late for their plane." Lou chortled. "He has no idea that Hank's coined me *lead foot.*"

"Maybe it's a better plan anyway since we'd be driving again to the airport in the morning." From Allie's photograph on the family room wall, I could have sworn she winked at me. "Besides, Allie and I already said our goodbyes." A sneak surprise lump caught in my throat. "Once is enough for this mama bear."

Chapter Forty

Lou ~ Paradise Found

Burying toes in sand, eyes closed, and listening to the tide roll in does wonders for the soul.

"We're on island time, baby." Essie's skin took on a golden glow through my aviator Ray-Bans—my go-to sunglasses well before all the Hollywood mavens and style-conscious youngsters started wearing them.

We'd enjoyed a fruit-laden, poolside breakfast early in the morning, and now my wife and I had navigated the red earth pathway down to the beach. The woven straw bag brimmed with suntan lotion, snacks, a once floppy but now smashed beach hat, and a couple of books—life's essentials when the only thing beneath your feet is fine grain sand.

"I could live here," Essie remarked, hand perched above her eyes to shield the glaring sun. "Could you?"

The thought was intriguing—leave the fast-paced life behind. But who was I kidding? The earned Golden Years were laced with truth—kids raised, career complete, and now time ebbed and flowed in its own dance.

"Living here permanently … I don't know. It's breathtaking, the air is fresh, and sea level is friendlier to the heart."

A spectacular view lay out before me. A meandering beach and a backdrop of greenery that blanketed the silent volcanic island rising above the majestic Pacific Ocean. Far in the distance, silhouettes of sailboats moved in slow motion. Closer to shore, boarders methodically paddled over bumps and valleys—floating on water as the ancient Hawaiians once did.

"Well, the nice thing is we don't have to decide." Essie leaned back into the low beach chair and settled glasses on her pink-tinged nose. "We have a perfect little house to return to and call home."

"Then we'll call ourselves fortunate—two paradises found."

* * * * *

A combination of the warmth of the sun, the lull of the ocean, and a morning mimosa must have rocked me to sleep. Groggily, I reached my hand toward Essie's lounge chair but found only a striped beach towel and her sunglasses.

"Lou, come join me," she called from the water. "Feels wonderful, and it's not too deep."

A landlubber at heart, I'd long ago made an agreement with the ocean. Like a faithful theatergoer, I watched and enjoyed as she performed on a vast and dramatic stage.

"A school of fish is swimming around my legs." My forever-young-at-heart wife squealed with delight. "They're not scared of me a bit."

Someone should invent a La-Z-Boy beach chair, one that could launch seniors to a stand. Dismounting was easier by rolling to the side. "There's an idea that could make me rich," I muttered.

Admittedly, the water was a welcome relief from the intensifying heat of the sand. It bobbed and splashed around my calves, then thighs and waist as I waded a little deeper.

"Try this." Essie spread her arms wide and flopped onto her back. "It's been a while since I've been this light."

"An illusion, my dear. The saltwater is lifting you up."

She splashed me and then relaxed into the sea—head back, hair swaying as though cradled in the arms of God—peaceful, protected, and free.

Slowly, I relinquished myself to the sea—struggling at first to trust it would support me, and then letting go. Face to the sky, my tummy protruding above the waterline so I resembled a baby humpback whale, the water held me.

Suddenly, the spell was broken by the reverberating sound of an approaching jet ski. The once soothing massage of the ocean sent a wave of water across my face. Coughing up a mouthful of salty water, underused abdominals and hamstrings helped my feet find the ground.

I spun around to find Essie ... but she was gone.

"Ess!" I yelled. "Where are you?"

A couple swimming nearby stopped, the man grabbing my arm. "What's wrong?"

"My wife …" I stammered. "She was just here. I can't find her." Panic overtook me, the same sickening feeling of losing one's child in a crowd.

"Is that her over there?" The woman pointed toward the beach.

"Yes, there she is." Like a goofy schoolboy, I thanked them and then half swam, half ran to the shallower waters. She was on her knees, bent forward with hair masked over part of her face.

"You all right?" I slumped next to her where the water briefly met the land and then receded as quickly as it had come. "Thought something awful happened to you."

Her initial reply was a cough and a gag, followed by a trickle of water from her trembling mouth.

"Lou … that really scared me." She held on to my arm, and we pushed to a stand. "Everything was so peaceful, like I was in heaven, floating on a cloud until a wave knocked me off."

"Me too, but looks like you took the brunt of it." A small welt was beginning to rise on her forehead. "You must have hit the bottom when the wake tossed you around."

She touched the wound and flinched. "Must have … but I'm okay now. Luckily, the wave pushed me to shore instead of out to sea."

I shuddered at the thought. Above, the ocean appeared inviting and calm, but beneath it was dark and foreboding. Fortunately, this time, instead of taking, the sea had delivered another gift.

"Hey, Essie, not that either one of us needs such a dramatic reminder"—my heart rate had finally returned to normal—"but we've been around long enough to know life will always have its sunrises and sunsets. My hope for us is to—"

"Find the beauty in both?"

I smiled. "Yes, in both."

Back at the chairs, I wrapped us in towels and settled on firm land.

"Can you hand me my book?" She smoothed her hair back, wincing at the tender spot on her forehead. "I found the perfect one to bring along, an old favorite of mine."

Digging for a moment in the bag, my hand found her gem.

"*Gift from the Sea*." I read the title. "How apropos."

"Anne Morrow Lindbergh knew what she was talking about when she penned this book. To her credit, I've reread this book time and time again at different stages in my life and …"

I waited for her to finish her thought.

"It always speaks to me." She sighed, running her hand gently over the cover. "I love that about a good book."

Rummaging under Ritz crackers and squished turkey sandwiches we'd commandeered from the resort buffet line, my book emerged.

"And what are you reading, dear?" Her eyebrows peeked above her sunglass rims. "How did you pack that thing into your suitcase? It alone would have tipped the scale over the fifty-pound limit."

I propped the hefty book on my knees. "William Shirer's, *The Rise and Fall of the Third Reich.* A classic."

"So I see." She returned to her book. "And fitting for you, Lou ... perfectly fitting."

Despite sunscreen smudges on my lenses, I flipped to the introduction and stepped onto history's path—ironically, one I'd journeyed on.

But before I ventured too far, Essie's sweet voice reminded me, "Honey, if you plan on getting through that entire book on our vacation, we may have to consider staying here a whole lot longer."

* * * * *

Because you can do that sort of thing when you're footloose and fancy-free, we extended our honeymoon two weeks longer.

Island time yawned a bit wider as we gazed at the late afternoon sun, casting defining shadows on the out-of-this world, Na Pali coastline.

Nestled in the largest inlet along the north shore, we strolled along Hanalei Bay for the fourth, fifth, maybe hundredth time. It didn't really matter, and it never got old.

My gaze, as always, found a place to rest as I lifted my eyes to the towering land before me. "Hard to imagine the mountains are eroding away." Undulations, like waves dropped from heaven, created curvy lines, stretching from towering, cascading waterfall cliffs, all the way to the ocean. "Someday, maybe hundreds or thousands of years from now when we are long gone ... this island will have washed away, returned to sea."

"That's sad for those who never get to experience this place." Essie tugged my hand and led me along the concrete pier toward the iconic ending point that stretched into the bay where picturesque boats awaited their next voyage.

"You know that book I've been rereading?" She stood with bare toes wiggling over the edge of the pier. "A part struck me this time like never before."

Facing forward, waiting to say goodbye to the soon-to-be setting sun, she recited Lindbergh's words. "We find again some of the joy in the now, some of the peace in the here, some of the love in me and thee"—I held her hand, and then she continued—"which go to make up the kingdom of heaven and earth."

Magically, colors painted themselves across the sky, a spectacular performance, if not for everyone, then at least for us.

Chapter Forty-One

Essie ~ By the Light of the Silvery Moon

It's always hard to say goodbye to paradise, but returning home has benefits too, like settling into a comfy chair—once you get in, you don't want to get out.

Summer was waning, a reminder that it would be nearly a year since Lou and I met. With that, the leaves were already tinged with color, and before long, the highest mountains would be wearing white caps.

Sleep was usually a welcome bedfellow. Tonight, it was elusive. As Lou lightly snored, I slid out of bed and padded down the hallway to the enclosed sunporch, dim and shadowy in the moonlight.

For the next several hours, my companions would be my brushes and paints. At Lou's insistence, when we'd moved into our small house, the most naturally lit room became my art studio. Now, in the middle of the night, it was surprisingly peaceful and calming.

I flicked on the gooseneck lamp, and as I surveyed the room and pondered what to paint, I quietly sang the chorus from a favorite old song, "By the Light of the Silvery Moon." Several tropical, honeymoon-inspired, partially completed canvases leaned against the wall. But tonight, none of those contained the inspiration to capture my soul.

I was about to give up, maybe try to read or watch TV until my eyesight blurred. But just before I switched off the lights, my attention was caught.

Lou must have positioned them on the paint supply table. Twin, glass containers—one holding white and the other shades of brown and gray—salt and pepper shakers sat side by side. They appeared out of place, nestled between jars of brushes and squished tubes of paint. But the way they stood steadfastly at each other's side, they were complete together—salt with its pepper and pepper with salt. I picked up my brush.

* * * * *

Morning came quickly after I had retired from my easel well past two. After a second cup of coffee, I was ready to surprise Lou with the gift. I ran a comb through my disheveled hair and inspected dark circles under my eyes. Didn't really matter. The twelve-by-twelve-inch, acrylic on canvas painting was a labor of love—a still life of salt and pepper shakers. I'd chosen the hues carefully, the objects painted shiny and silver, highlighted with surprising accents of color—lights and darks adding perspective and depth—just as our lives had evolved.

When Lou padded into the kitchen in robe and slippers, he greeted me with a good morning kiss and then stared at the small painting propped on the table against the vase filled with sunflowers. He didn't say anything at first, but instead lifted the canvas and held it to his chest.

"Essie, it's perfect." He smiled. "It's …"

"Us," we said.

Now, each morning, Lou and I are greeted by the painting. It hangs on the wall in a prime position next to our kitchen table—joining us for breakfast, lunch, dinner, and whatever snacks fall in between.

To some, the subject might be simplistic, perhaps unimportant, and easy to overlook. But for us, the salt and pepper shakers are symbolic—seasoned with the past, present, and future, and most importantly, the here and the now.